*The Villain of the Earth*

# The Villain of the Earth

## SIMON SHAW

St. Martin's Press
New York

**M**

Library of Congress Cataloging-in-Publication Data

Shaw, Simon.
    The villain of the earth / Simon Shaw.
        p.      cm.
    "A Thomas Dunne book."
    ISBN 0-312-13201-8
    PR6069.H3948V55    1995
    823'.914—dc20
                                                95-1757
                                                CIP

First published in Great Britain by Victor Gollancz Ltd.

First U.S. Edition: June 1995
10  9  8  7  6  5  4  3  2  1

I am alone the villain of the earth,
And feel I am so most.

*Antony and Cleopatra*, IV, vi.

*The Villain of the Earth*

'Come on, luvvies, I've got an interview at four . . .'

Philip Fletcher ground out the butt of his cigarette in the nasty plastic ashtray provided. His co-star for the morning, the celebrated light comedy actress Angela Rose, looked at her watch.

'You've got six hours,' she offered, with attempted soothing blandness.

'It'll be six bloody weeks the rate he's going,' Philip muttered back. He lit another cigarette. 'For Christ's sake, what's he doing now?'

Philip made a broad rhetorical gesture of despair in the direction of the set.

They were on one of the major sound stages at Pinewood Studios, a vast shell of a building in which it was impossible not to be reminded of a hangar, though in truth a whole aeroplane factory might have been accommodated comfortably. In one corner stood a simulacrum of the kind of hi-tech kitchen one usually only encounters in the homes of interviewees in *Hello* magazine. A spindly young man in torn jeans and a ponytail was squatting under the spotless gleaming table and peering out earnestly through a hand-held lens.

'Getting his angles right, dear,' said Angela indifferently.

'He's got more sodding angles than Pythagoras.'

'Well, you know what young directors are like these days. He is meant to be a bit of a perfectionist.'

'Angela, this isn't the sequel to *Last Year at Marienbad*. It's a bloody coffee commercial.'

The director had summoned over the designer. A snippet of their conversation wafted across.

'It's the reflection from the coffee pot. I'm not getting metal, I'm somehow getting ceramic.'

'I'd call it getting pretentious, dear,' Angela murmured. Philip scoffed.

'Who does he think he is?'

'Ridley Scott?' Angela suggested, after a moment's thought.

Philip sighed. She was right, of course. The days when TV advertisements had been the province of mere jobbing hacks were, as with so much else, long, long gone. Now they were the testing grounds of tyros crammed with film-school theories, of pop-video-suckled image fetishists looking for a leg-up on to the Hollywood gravy train. One Hovis ad later and there'd be real dollars for tea.

'What's the interview for?' Angela asked, not because she wanted to know (she sounded too bored to want to know anything), but to help fill in the gaps.

'Sorry?' said Philip, though he had heard perfectly – he was just preparing his ground.

'What are you going up for?'

'Oh . . .' Philip flipped his hand casually. 'Just another little old Shakespeare . . . *Antony and Cleopatra*.'

'Oh yes, I read about that in the *Guardian*. That dreadful chap Shitski's directing, isn't he?'

'Who?'

'You know, the Russian, whatsisname . . . Sergei Shustikov I think's his real name. I don't know, everyone calls him Shitski, meant to be a real monster. Are you sure you're up to it?'

Philip stared at her carefully. She did have a reputation for being a little daffy, but she seemed to have got her wires crossed in a big way.

'No, I'm talking about *Antony and Cleopatra*,' he repeated slowly. 'It's being done at the National, or the Royal National as we're meant to say these days. Ben Ferris is directing actually.'

'Who?'

Philip sighed. It was obviously a complete waste of time trying to show off in front of her.

'Ben Ferris. Won the Olivier last time around. The new

hot-shot whizz kid. Rather flattering he wants to see me, of course.'

'Which part are you up for?'

'I'll give you a clue. It isn't Cleopatra.'

He didn't tell her that he was only being seen because a theatrical knight had dropped out at the last minute; he saw no need to go into unnecessary detail. Angela was having enough difficulty taking it in already.

'Oh, really?' she said uncertainly. 'So it isn't the Shitski one?'

'No, Angela, it is not.'

'Oh. Funny though, isn't it? Two productions of the same play on at exactly the same time. Bit of a coincidence, eh?'

'Only a bit. A few years back there were three *Tempest*s on in London simultaneously. The year after I think we got a flock of *Lear*s. If, as Hitchcock observed, actors are cattle, then directors are undoubtedly sheep. Do you think we are ever going to get called, or are we doomed to sit in these rather uncomfortable canvas chairs for the rest of eternity?'

Angela shrugged. Conversation dried up and a state of blissless lassitude engulfed them. When finally they were called Philip came round sluggishly, like the Beast from Twenty Thousand Fathoms loosed from his icy tomb. A coffee helped revive him. As a commodity it was not in short supply.

'All right, everyone,' said the director at last, 'let's go for a take.'

They prepared to do a master shot. Philip assumed his position by the kitchen table. Angela framed herself in the doorway. After a few more pointless lapses of time they received their cue.

'What's happened to us?' Angela demanded with quivering, splendid intensity. 'Why do you never talk to me any more?'

'I'm sorry, darling,' Philip murmured back darkly, holding his steaming mug of coffee to his breast, '. . . but you'll never understand.'

Angela stifled a sob.

'It's all you ever think of, isn't it? Coffee!'

Philip took a sip of the offending liquid (it was quite revolting) and smiled contentedly.

'Coffee! Coffee! Coffee!' Angela whimpered. Philip looked pained.

'Oh no, dear, not just any coffee . . .' He lifted the mug obliquely to the camera. 'It's Ebony Smooth. There is a difference . . .'

He turned his profile three-quarters on and gave his deepest, smuggest smile. Angela spun on her heels and stormed out, overacting loudly but harmlessly. While Philip stood majestically in the foreground, all the sound was going to be faded out for the voice-over and final plug:

'Taste the difference. Ebony Smooth.'

Hardly a humdinger as captions went, but what did it matter? It was all a complete load of balls anyway.

'Cut,' said the director thoughtfully. He came and stood in front of Philip. He was wearing his favourite expression, one more readily suited in Philip's eye to the subject of constipation than caffeine.

'Erotic!' he exclaimed suddenly, after a protracted mental fumble.

'I'm sorry?' said Philip, who feared that he might soon have cause to be. The director nodded his head emphatically.

'I want more sex!'

Philip smiled pleasantly.

'Don't we all, but I'm not sure you're my type.'

In other circumstances Philip's levity might have been dangerous, but the agonized auteur simply ignored his remark.

'When you look at the coffee, it's got to be like you're getting a hard-on.'

'I see.'

'That's why she's so pissed off with you, right? It's the classic sexual triangle. She wants you, but you want the coffee.'

'What does the coffee want?'

'That's not important. She's got the hump because you're giving her the cold shoulder.'

'Because I'd rather have a hot coffee?'

'Really *have* it, you know what I mean?'

'A case of stuff her, I want to screw the coffee?'

'Yeah. Literally.'

'Literally? Mm, I wonder what market you're aiming at exactly . . .'

Philip turned to Angela, who had put on an expression of polite but strained indulgence, in the manner of Joyce Grenfell. 'I bet this never happened to the Gold Blend couple.'

'Just think of the repeat fees,' she murmured back, *sotto voce*.

He'd been thinking about little else all day. What he really interested in was her fees, which he suspected would come to rather more than his, but, like the experienced old pro that she was, she had deflected his most incisive probes. Not that he had anything to complain of; he was merely curious.

He had turned down the option of residuals in favour of a buy-out, a cool lump-sum payment of £25,000. As remuneration for one day's work it was hardly for sniffing at, but it didn't begin to compare with the kind of sums big stars could command. Had he been currently appearing in a popular TV series – as was Angela – then he could have expected more, but his own bubble-brand of celebrity, despite recent near-puncturings, was still more or less lodged at the quality end of the market, where the rewards were appreciably less. He supposed that his appointment to the complex and sought-after role of 'husband with coffee mug' represented a touching attempt on the part of the advertisers to associate sophistication and taste with their largely disgusting product. For twenty-five big ones, he was prepared to surrender a modicum of integrity towards the greater cause of his bank balance. When it came down to it, very few actors weren't.

'Sorry about the delay,' said the assistant director, coming across to them. 'You've got time for a coffee, if you like.'

'I'm sick to death of the muck,' said Philip. 'He does realize, I hope, that he's only got me till three. I've an interview in town.'

'Oh?' The assistant looked mildly interested. 'Anything good?'

'He's going up for *Antony and Cleopatra*,' Angela answered for him. 'He's a proper posh actor is our Philip.'

'Yeah?' The assistant looked mildly impressed. 'I heard about that. He's meant to be a bit of a bastard, right?'

'Who is?'

'That Russian. Shit-face, or whatever he's called.'

'Is that so?' Philip answered crossly. 'Then it's just as well that I shan't be having anything to do with him...'

Philip's temper did not improve as the long morning dragged laboriously on. He had been hoping to have a break before his interview, but the constant fussing and retaking of shots ate inexorably into the afternoon, and by the time he had finished gazing lustfully into the obsidian depths of his mug for the last close-up there was no leeway left at all. He bid a hurried adieu to Angela, wriggled out of his clothes on the run, and after a lightning change and a perfunctory dab at his make-up, threw himself dramatically into the back of the waiting car. With Philip's earnest plea for speed humming in his ears, the driver zoomed off towards the motorway.

They made it to the stage door of the National with two minutes to spare. After taking a few deep breaths for composition's sake, Philip exited smartly from the car and sailed in through the plate-glass swing-doors like a clipper in full flight. He dropped anchor grandly in front of the reception desk.

'I'm here to see Ben Ferris,' he announced to the assembled mechanicals.

The woman in front of him glanced indifferently at a typed sheet of paper.

'Are you Stewart McCoist?'

'Och aye the noo,' replied Philip grimly. Although he did not recognize any of the staff currently on duty it had been only two years since he had given his all for his art under this very same roof. He enunciated crisply: 'I am Philip Fletcher.'

The woman nodded and picked up a phone. Clearly that cluster-bomb of proper nouns had set off no tremors in her subconscious.

'Sign in, please,' she said, indicating an open book on the other side of the desk. One of her confrères offered him a pen and he neatly curled his signature. A third handed him a plastic badge and requested him to wait. Philip found it oddly reassuring, after a decade of Thatcherism, to find evidence of East European manning levels still flourishing.

He sat down reluctantly in one of the semi-comfortable chairs beside the all-glass doors. He always hated sitting there. Not only was it like being in a goldfish bowl, it was also one of the worst places in London for running into people one would normally cross not merely the street, but a full double page of the A–Z, to avoid. He lifted his collar and folded his chin in his scarf.

'Philip? Hi!'

Philip looked up in some surprise. On the other side of reception a fair sprightly teenager was standing over an elderly character actor with a vaguely familiar face. The face was wearing a blank expression.

'It is Philip Fletcher, isn't it?' said the teenager to the elderly actor.

'That's not what it says in *Spotlight*,' he replied evenly. Simultaneously they both turned and looked at the real Philip, who happened to be the only other person waiting.

'Yes, it is me . . .' he intoned in a clipped monotone, his smile as thin as his voice. 'Wearing a more brilliant disguise than even I had realized.'

'Great!' said the grinning teenager, not seeming remotely put out by his gaffe. He turned his back on the False Philip and offered a thin white paw. 'I'm Ben.'

'So I surmised.'

'Right. Let's go.'

They went out past the desk into the corridor. They headed for the lifts.

'Mind if we stop off in the canteen?' enquired Ben Ferris pleasantly. 'Been seeing people all day – I'm ravenous!'

His spare frame looked insufficient to bear the ravages of appetite. Mind you, Philip thought, that sandy mane and freckled mien looked better suited, far, to the demands of a scout hut than to the exigencies of life in the cultural bunker.

Where do they come from? Philip wondered to himself.

'Sorry?' said the young man.

'Um, nothing . . .' Philip gave a poorly improvised cough. He had meant to be keeping his wondering to himself; speaking his thoughts aloud was a dangerous habit.

The lift pinged and the door took its slow electric age to open. Ben Ferris ushered Philip in.

'Shall we go up then?'

And up they went, not merely into the canteen, but into the heady realms of theatrical legend.

Later that night, after curtain down, two actors were sitting in a corner of the National's backstage bar, having a drink and a chat.

Of course the room was full of actors, many still on that high of nervous energy which makes the profession a night-breed, but these two, a pair of old troupers if ever there was, sat apart, one nursing a port and lemon, the other a Guinness with a raspberry top.

'Lovely performance, dear,' said the port drinker, who was just visiting the concrete Shrine of Art. 'Or did I tell you that already?'

The Guinness quaffer grunted phlegmatically.

'Yes, you did, but it offends me not to hear you oft repeat it. Speak again, Bright Angel.'

'Happy to oblige. Once more for luck – lovely perf! Despite your being marooned throughout Act II on the Gobi desert of the Olivier stage.'

'Don't . . . Could you hear all right?'

'You and the oldies. The youngsters were inaudible beyond the third row, as per usual. Are my eyes deceiving me, or is that Dick Jones over there?'

'Where?'

'At the bar. In the loud embroidered shirt. He's not queer, is he?'

'No. I mean yes. I mean, that is him, but he's not queer.'

'Mm, you never can tell. Is he a friend of yours?'

'An acquaintance. Why, do you want to meet him?'

'No, it's just that in the circumstances I'm mildly interested.'

'Oh yes, of course, all those *Antony and Cleo*s. If I catch his eye, I'll get him over. By the way . . . you know Philip Fletcher, don't you?'

'Yes. Why?'

'Is he a friend of yours?'

'Mm, I'm not sure Philip has friends. We've always got on well enough, though. Why are you asking?'

'Because he was here earlier today. Throwing a wobbly.'

'Really? Ooh, tell me more!'

'Well, it's all rather a coincidence actually. You see, I don't know him, except by reputation, but I'd just come in at the stage door, and there I was minding my own business – in fact I was waiting for a buzz from Front of House to confirm they'd booked your ticket – when who should come sauntering over to me but Ben Ferris, cool as you please, saying "Philip Fletcher, I presume," like Spencer Tracy bursting out of the bush.'

'You bear about as much resemblance to Philip Fletcher as I do to Katharine Hepburn.'

'Slightly less, I'd say. Anyway, in other circumstances I might have been amused, but it's not as if I'm nobody, is it? I've even met Ben Ferris, here in the bar, we've been properly introduced.'

'Maybe he's suffering from juvenile dementia. You must have been annoyed.'

'I was. But not as much as Philip Fletcher.'

'You don't mean . . . Good God! Was he there? I'm not surprised he threw a wobbly!'

'Oh no, the wobbly came later. He took it quite well actually. He was rather dry.'

'That sounds like our Philip. Toasty, with extra crust. So where did the screaming habdabs come in?'

'About ten minutes later, up in the canteen. I just popped in for a coffee on my way to the dressing room and there they were in the corner. And, my dear, you should have heard the language! It was like that Barrie Keefe play I was in at the Court.'

'That bad? Mm, he must have been upset. Did you hear what they were saying?'

'I certainly heard every word he said. I must say, his diction's well up to par.'

'You mean he might even be heard on the Olivier stage?'

'And that, my dear old chum, was precisely the point at issue ... Your drink's dipped well below the Plimsoll line. My round, isn't it?'

'That's as may be, but you're not going anywhere – Come on, I'm on tenterhooks! What was the point at issue?'

'*Antony and Cleopatra*. I mean, the one they're doing here, of course. Only it was coming over more like *The Comedy of Errors*. Or perhaps it was more Ben Travers—'

'Yes, yes, forgive me for butting in, old thing, but I do have to say you're not explaining this awfully well. So far I've got that Philip has come in to talk to Ferris. What's so odd about that?'

'Only this: Fletcher was under the impression he was being seen for Antony.'

'What? Don't be ridiculous! Everyone in London knows Dick Jones is playing Antony.'

'Everyone, it would appear, except Philip Fletcher.'

'I see. And that was when he threw the wobbly? Why was Ferris seeing him then?'

'For your part. Enobarbus.'

'Enobarbus? Are you joking?'

'That was Fletcher's reaction. Well, what he said was, and I quote, "Eno-fucking-barbus, are you out of your tiny fucking skull?"'

'I see what you mean about the language. Mind you, it's understandable. Do you suppose Ben Ferris has read the play?'

'Maybe, maybe not. Who can tell these days? I think he thought Fletcher was older than he is.'

'Philip must have been miffed about that too. He's as vain as a prima donna. He spends half his life looking in the mirror.'

'Show me a thesp who doesn't. He is a good actor though, isn't he?'

'Oh yes, he's good. Not as good as he thinks he is, of course, but I don't suppose Kean or Garrick were quite as good as Philip thinks he is. Go on. What happened next?'

'Well, it might have been all right, but unfortunately Ben Ferris tried to apologize. Fletcher had got himself back under control and was obviously engaged in damage limitation – I mean, when he blew up everyone just stopped dead and looked at him, and it must have been obvious we'd all been eavesdropping before that, so Fletcher must have felt pretty humiliated, and I could see him setting his jaw and putting his head down and preparing for a swift and decisive exit pursued by a bear – you know, get it over with. Probably would have gone straight out and hurled himself off Waterloo bridge the state he was in. But Ferris just wouldn't let go.'

'What was he saying?'

'Well, he was trying to explain that it wasn't his fault, his instructions to the casting people had been clear. Not that you can believe a word of that, the casting's been a complete cock-up from start to finish, or so I've heard. Anyway, Ferris is just fishing desperately for excuses. What did your agent tell you? he asks, to which Fletcher hisses: "Don't speak ill of the dead!"'

'Good line, that. Wish I'd said it.'

'You will, dear, you will. "Nice to meet you!" mutters Fletcher with barely controlled fury, spinning on his heels and turning to the door, but that's when Ferris plays his joker. He says, with absolute and fatal clarity: "I've just had a thought, would you like to play Pompey?"'

'*Quel* thought! Ooh, cringe, cringe!'

'I'll say. What makes it worse is that he obviously thought he was being helpful. "Would I fucking well what?" gasps Fletcher, all pretence at self-control sent packing out of the window. And that was when his wobbly went thermo-nuclear. Are you sure you don't want another drink?'

'Are you mad? Get on with it!'

'Just teasing ... Well, imagine the scene: Ferris has just fired his cruise missile and a deathly hush has descended on the once-busy canteen. Not a whisper was heard, not even the scraping of a teaspoon on a china mug—'

'Yes, yes, stop hamming it up. What did Fletcher do?'

'He exploded. I don't know about railing against the firstborn of Egypt, this was the full *King Lear* treatment, Act III, scene ii. "How effing dare you!" he screams. "Who the effing hell do you effing well think you effing are?" '

'Doesn't sound effing Shakespearian to me.'

'It was the modern-dress version. You pimply pile of freeze-dried bat droppings.'

'Who serrated your tongue this morning?'

'No, not you. That's what Fletcher said to Ferris. You camp old tart.'

'Fletcher said that to Ferris?'

'No, I'm saying it to you, you daft old queen. Fletcher called Ferris a pre-pubescent pig-ignorant shit-bag.'

'Nice.'

'And told him he was a talentless, tactless, mosquito-brained vulgarian who didn't know the difference between art and his arsehole.'

'Cruel. But essentially accurate.'

'And furthermore, that he was a jammy, jumped-up little jerk who knew as much about the theatre as the England cricket selectors knew about cricket.'

'Ooh, nasty!'

'I know. That one must have really struck home. Poor Ferris was bright maroon by this stage, I felt almost sorry for him. But Fletcher hadn't finished yet.'

'What did he say next?'

'I'm afraid this is where it did get rather incoherent. Fletcher's ranting rose to fever pitch and it all got a bit Method – you know, all noise, no sense. Very impressive, though. Ben Ferris just sat there looking like a turkey on Boxing Day. I thought Fletcher was going to wallop him.'

'Did he?'

'No, he just spun on his heels and turned away smartly. All eyes were upon him, of course, it was quite an exit. And just as he's going out this other actor comes in who I don't know but he's obviously a friend of Fletcher's, and this chap says all chirpily, "Hello, Philip, old man, what brings you here?" and Fletcher pauses, fixes Ferris with a baleful eye and then, with the deadliest, coolest delivery I think I've ever heard, says,

"I was led to believe there was a theatre company operating somewhere within this godforsaken bombsite of a building. I must have been mistaken." Exit.'

'Lights. Curtain. Thunderous applause.'

'I have to admit I could barely refrain from clapping. It was a great deal more exciting than anything we've done on stage here recently.'

'Mm, how extraordinary. Mind you, Philip Fletcher is full of surprises. I remember him getting into a violent contretemps like that with Richie Calvi in Bath.'

'Oh yes, I'd forgotten you were in on that. Fletcher was involved in a few bust-ups there, wasn't he?'

'I'll say. Somehow he always seems to be in the thick of the action. You know he was in that film which folded, the one where the producer and that soap actress were found dead together?'

'Oh yes. Ken Kilmaine and Shelley Lamour.'

'And he was a key witness when they were investigating poor old Gordon Wilde's murder. Having Philip around is a bit like working with the Angel of Death. And he was such a quiet boy when I first knew him.'

'Probably a good thing he's not coming here after all then.'

'A good thing who isn't coming here after all?' enquired a deep, melodious third voice, butting in.

'Ah!' said the Guinness drinker. 'Talk of the devil. Do you two know each other? Richard Jones. Seymour Loseby.'

Seymour Loseby smiled coyly at the owner of the loud embroidered shirt. His own garb was scarcely less colourful.

'Known by reputation. Will you join us? What we were discussing touches on you.'

'Oh?' Dick Jones pulled up a chair from the next table. 'And what was that?'

The Guinness drinker leant across conspiratorially.

'I was just telling him about Philip Fletcher's little fracas in the canteen.'

'Ah yes. Quite embarrassing for me really.'

He neither looked nor sounded embarrassed. Rather, his glee was only just on the leash.

'Poor Philip!'

He laughed. His concern did not seem unduly overdone.

'Seymour's quite a chum of his, you know,' said the Guinness drinker, letting off a mild parting shot.

'Well, we've worked together once or twice,' interjected Seymour smoothly, rubbing his palms together in the manner of Pontius Pilate. 'Actually, I was with him when he had that dreadful flop on Broadway.'

'Oh yes,' responded Dick Jones, putting on a pained expression. 'Rather unfortunate that, wasn't it?'

'Rather. I'm not the superstitious type, you know, but as I was saying before you joined us, our Philip just might be the teensiest weensiest bit jinxed.'

'Are you sure it's not you who's jinxed?' asked the Guinness drinker slyly. He gave Dick Jones a nudge. 'He's in the other *Cleopatra*, you know.'

'Oh, Shustikov's production? How fascinating ... Of course, I have the greatest respect for Ian—'

'I'm sure you have, but he's not playing Antony any more.'

'What? I don't understand. Shustikov was in the paper the other day saying how much he was looking forward to working with Ian—'

'And in today's paper they've busted up. Didn't you see the *Standard*? Tell him, Seymour.'

'I'm afraid it's true,' said Seymour. 'I don't know much about it, but apparently they've split up over artistic differences.'

'Ha!' His friend laughed cynically. 'That old chestnut!'

'I see ...' Dick Jones looked thoughtful. 'What a pity. I was looking forward to measuring myself against Ian. Hadn't you started rehearsals?'

'No, we're due to begin in a fortnight, just after you. It's all a bit of a coincidence, really.'

'What do you mean?'

'Well ...' Seymour spread his hands innocently. 'Didn't something rather like that happen here? I mean, you weren't the original choice for the part, were you, Dick?'

Dick Jones smiled thinly.

'All swings and roundabouts in this business, boyo. Is your production going to fold then?'

'Oh no, they can't afford for that to happen. Shitski's looking for another Antony.'

'Really? Not going to be easy, this late, is it?'

Seymour Loseby smiled mischievously.

'Well, Philip Fletcher's available, isn't he?'

*3*

Philip rarely entered the upstairs rooms in his flat. He used the study for the occasional bit of typing, but had hardly even crossed the threshold of the spare bedroom in the last two years. It was a small, dark room, impossible to heat or light properly. He went almost immediately up to it on his return from the Royal National Theatre, stopping off only briefly in the kitchen to collect a hammer and a bag of nails. He put them in a carrier bag with the purchases he had just made in Upper Street, and climbed the spiral iron staircase. For the next half hour he did a vigorous if implausible impersonation of a do-it-yourself enthusiast. Then he went downstairs, changed into a black polo-neck and matching trousers and opened a bottle of red wine. He drank half of the bottle while listening to his personal reel-to-reel selection of Wagnerian highlights. After chain-smoking half a dozen cigarettes and dousing his ire with Flagstad and Furtwängler he felt sufficiently calmed to think clearly. It was dark now, he got up to close the curtains. Then he grabbed the bottle of wine and went back upstairs.

There was an alcove in the corner of the small bedroom which contained a sink. It was here that he had worked earlier, constructing a makeshift board which he had balanced on the taps, and an improvised curtain, a black strip of velvet which hung down from a poorly fitted rail. He opened the curtain and lit the seven candles on the board. Then he turned off the main light and shut the door. He returned to the sink and knelt on the floor before it, clasping the enamel sides for support.

'Thou, Revenge, art my Goddess . . .'

The candlelight flickered against the dusty wall tiles; it

glinted in the glass of the mirror above. Philip's voice boomed around the narrow alcove; it was a harsh acoustic.

'Revenge my Goddess. Revenge and her three minions, Rage, Loathing and Contempt. My Furies, my three ill-Graces. Hear me, O Goddess. Come, Ate, hot from hell, with Retribution in your train!'

Between the candles, stood against the wall, were two small dolls, fresh from their toyshop plastic packaging. Philip opened the tin of dressmaker's pins and made a selection. With measured spite he addressed the first doll:

'Be thou called Ferris. Ben to your cretinous friends. May your days and nights be racked with hideous torments. And may you never win another theatrical award again, you talentless dull disc-jockey-brained sub-moron.'

He jabbed the pin into the doll's breast. The point penetrated the soft plastic easily. He picked up the bottle of wine and spilt liberal drops over the doll's head.

'Bleed, you bugger, bleed!'

The little stream trickled down the doll's torso and stained the wooden board between its feet. Philip selected another pin and drove it into the second doll.

'Be thou called Jones. Dick, an appropriate forename, you slimy repellent Welsh scumbag, with your prop forward's cauliflower face and your grating insidious lilting vowels. Richard the turd. Dick the prick. Jones the unspeakable. I had rather live with cheese and garlic in a windmill, far, than sit through a mere two minutes of one of your ghastly unimaginative arse-achingly boring epiglottis-tickling performances ever again, you barely humanoid half-hearted apology for a Celtic retard. Have another one on me, you bastard.'

Philip stuck in a gratuitous second pin, a half-inch above the first. He poured some more wine over the second doll, caught his breath, then intoned solemnly:

> Eye of Ben and toe of Dick
> I wonder who's the bigger prick?
> Let the cauldron boil and hiss
> With all that's loathsome in the biz.

Popstar's talent tinned in aspic
Liver of pretentious critic
Method actor's earnest tedium
Casting lady's cranial vacuum
Angry playwright's hollow speeches,
Journalists, assorted leeches,
Chat-show hosts awash with smarm
Producers lacking any charm
Crashing bores who can't take hints
Architects with wretched blueprints
Punters clapping in wrong places
Corporate sponsors' ugly faces
Agents' rank hypocrisy
Oscar winners who aren't me
All the creeps who make me sick
Above all Ben, above all Dick.
Throw in the cauldron all that's vile
Let it simmer – to taste add bile!

Philip's haunches were aching. He stood and stretched his legs. He lit a cigarette.

'Feeling better?' he asked his reflection in the mirror above the sink.

His reflection nodded back.

'Not much, but some . . . It would have been humiliating enough whoever they'd got, but Dick Jones!'

He winced. He snatched the wine bottle up off the floor and took a hearty swig. Whisky was what he really needed. He really needed to get plastered.

'Dick revolting Jones . . . Of all the lower life-forms in the universe, why oh why did Ben Ferris have to select that one? And why did nobody tell me? What on earth's going on? What sort of an operation are they running there these days? Is there anyone in London who can tell me what the fuck's happening? What's my agent been playing at? You're dead meat, Quennell, you've screwed it up one time too many. Jones for Antony – Christ! I can't believe it! I wouldn't cast him as the snake in Act V. I'll murder the little shit . . .'

Why hadn't he murdered him years ago? He was a nasty piece of work. If any one Equity member deserved the chop that person was Dick Jones.

'I thought about it, though, didn't I? Oh yes, I remember, when we were both up for Walter Raleigh and you were second choice. You knew you were second choice too, didn't you? I saw the way you looked at me in the BBC canteen. "Well done!" you said. "Let me buy you a coffee." Like Lady Macbeth offering Duncan a top-up. You'd have slipped something in if I'd given you the chance. Just as well I declined. I saw through you, you slime-ball. Always have done, always, always, always. Since Bristol.'

They'd been together in Manchester before that, but it had been only for one play and they'd hardly spoken. In Bristol they had shared a dressing room throughout the season. It had been fifteen years ago.

'Nastiest little creep I ever shared a mirror with. I know it was you who nicked my carmine grease stick. Never admitted it though, did you? Too mean even to buy your own. Couldn't even get your own girlfriend . . .'

Philip took a last, lung-plumbing drag of his cigarette, then stubbed it out in the face of the right-hand doll.

'Couldn't even be bothered to take her back to your place, could you, you cheap tacky bastard?'

They had both been playing the bailiffs' men in the end-of-season pantomime. They were always called together, Jones had known he'd be in the theatre. That was why he'd done it.

'I'll never forget it, never been so humiliated. I walked into the dressing room and there you were, having her in the corner. And it was my bloody corner! You didn't even have the good taste to lock the door.'

Philip lit another cigarette and smoked on it deeply. He frowned at the mirror. What had she been called? She was one of the dancers, local girl, dim but randy, a rare oasis in the sexual desert that had been his early thirties. It hadn't been serious between them, but that wasn't the point. Jones had only done it to spite him.

'At least you never got into Natasha's knickers.'

On the other hand, nor had he. He'd only got off with the dancer because Natasha Fielding had turned him down. Natasha had been the star of the season, and principal boy in the panto. Thank God she'd rejected Jones too. She'd spurned all of them, except the director.

'Why do directors always get the pretty ones?'

He glowered at the left-hand doll. He gave the pin in its breast a tweak. Ferris was only an irritation, but Jones was a recurring nightmare in his life. Only last year he'd beaten him to a major TV role. Actually, it had been worse than that – the bastard producers hadn't even seen Philip for the part. It was that series which had made Jones suddenly hot, after a topsy-turvy and largely lukewarm career. He'd gone straight afterwards to Stratford to do one show and suddenly everyone had started referring to him as a 'major Shakespearian actor'. Of course, standards at Stratford had fallen dramatically, but even so, it was enough to make anyone puke.

'God, I need a drink.'

Not wine, that wouldn't do at all, but he didn't have any Scotch. He'd been so good the last few months, he'd been as near as dammit on the wagon. He was even girding his loins for another attempt on his nicotine addiction. He took a rueful drag of his cigarette.

'Sod it. When you're this buggered to start with, what's the point?'

The corner shop would still be open. He should get something to eat, in any case. He closed the curtains on his voodoo shrine, climbed down the spiral staircase and put on his coat. He hurried across Highbury Fields.

'Anything else for you, Mr Fletcher?' asked Jim, the genial shop owner, putting twenty Rothmans and a bottle of Grouse into a bag for him.

'Mm . . .' Philip examined reluctantly the limited selection of unappetizing comestibles. He chose a pork pie and a bar of milk chocolate. He suspected that the meat content of the latter at least equalled that of the former.

'Oh yes, I want a paper.'

The car had come to pick him up at five that morning, he had neither read nor seen any news all day. He picked a *Standard* off the rack. Jim put the newspaper into the bag for him. He walked back home briskly.

The first Scotch went down almost unnoticed, the second began to soothe him. He pushed aside the half-eaten pork pie, broke open the chocolate bar and lit a cigarette. He stretched out in his armchair and let his thoughts drift away under their own steam.

'I've always wanted to blow up the National Theatre. Not a bad idea to take the Hayward and a few other hideous carbuncles along with it. How do I ensure Ferris and Jones are in there at the right time? Don't want to take too many innocent members of the public with them. Mind you, anyone who actually spends twenty quid of his own money to watch Jones act deserves to be blown to buggery. Why don't I just shoot the bastards? After all, I've got a gun, haven't I?'

Oh yes, he had a gun all right, the neat little black revolver with which Shelley Lamour had tried to kill him. It wasn't in the flat, of course; he kept it in a West End safe deposit box, along with the blackmail money he had extracted from the late unlamented Ken Kilmaine. He'd never used a gun in his life, but there were five bullets in the chamber. He should be able to hit Jones or Ferris with at least one of them.

'I'd better get a good alibi lined up. Plod will be beating a path to my door quicker than you can say fabricated confession.'

He sighed. That, unfortunately, was his problem: the police had such long memories. Gone were the days when he could dispose of his hated rivals with impunity. Ken Kilmaine was a case in point. At first, when they'd discovered his and Shelley's bodies, the police had asked Philip only routine questions. But then some bright spark had consulted the files and they'd come back yapping round his ankles like terriers on heat. They hadn't been as nasty as that wretched inspector in Bath – what was his name?

'Higginbottom . . .'

Ah yes, Chief Inspector Higginbottom. How could he have

forgotten? Well, they hadn't been as nasty as him, but they'd still been pretty damned awkward. The police, it appeared, were reluctant to forget him. Richie Calvi, Owen Trethowan, Harry Foster, Gordon Wilde ... What a memory they had for names! And they seemed to love making his life uncomfortable.

'No, it's only a matter of time before they find something to pin on me. If I blew away Ferris and Jones I'd just be playing into their hands. I'll have to think of another way of getting back at them. What a bloody nuisance it is being successful. I didn't have this trouble when I was a nonentity.'

He gave a sarcastic bray.

'Successful? Ha! I'm not exactly feeling bloody successful at the moment, am I?'

Still, it was better than it had been. Would he seriously have thought of swapping where he was now for where he'd been fifteen years ago – play-as-cast seasonal contract, seventy-five quid a week and the kind of digs that would have brought a protest from hardened lifers in the Scrubs? Digs like he'd had in Bristol ... He shuddered. Yes, he'd been younger then, but a fat lot of good it had done him. It was embarrassing to recall his failure-rate with women in those days. Worse than embarrassing. He'd behaved like a complete idiot over Natasha. To think of it still brought colour to his cheeks.

'Don't be silly,' he muttered to himself, refilling his glass. 'It was just puppy love.'

'Puppy love?' he muttered back incredulously. 'You were thirty-two! Always made a bloody fool of yourself over women, didn't you? Always played the green boy. Made the part your own. Learnt nothing and forgot nothing, like an amorous Bourbon. What a callow clumsy oaf you were. What a waste.'

He sighed. If his early thirties had been a sexual desert, his life now scarcely qualified as better than dry savannah. Fruitless as it was to dwell on lost opportunities, there was no other kind currently available.

'Ah, Natasha, Natasha, wherefore art thou, darling girl?'

She was in America, he seemed to recall. So what? No point in getting all nostalgic now. Nostalgic for what? It hadn't just been Natasha. He'd had more rejections than an experimental novelist.

He topped up his glass and burned his throat again with Scotch. He picked up the *Standard* and scanned the front page. Just the usual doom and gloom. He flicked through casually to the diary page. An ill-defined picture of a woman on the arm of an even fuzzier man caught his eye. He glanced idly at the caption:

NATASHA FIELDING – UP THE NILE WITHOUT A PADDLE?

'What?'

He literally fell out of his chair. He sat awkwardly on the carpet, his ankle caught uncomfortably under his leg, staring gormlessly at the paragraph under the photo.

The beautiful Natasha Fielding, pictured here last night with long-time boyfriend Sergei Shustikov leaving the Groucho Club, is reportedly devastated by Ian McIntyre's last-minute withdrawal from 'Antony & Cleopatra', due to begin rehearsals at the Riverside Studios in a fortnight. The fiery Shustikov, infamous for his furious temper, has denied reports of a violent bust-up, citing a difference of 'artistic opinion' as the cause of the split. The sultry Natasha (too long absent from our shores) said she was optimistic about finding a last-minute replacement to play opposite her Queen of the Nile, but Ian McIntyre's agent was a bit more doubt-ful when I spoke to him last night. 'I don't know how many masochistic actors there are left in London,' he said mysteriously. Unfortunately his client was unavailable for comment.

Philip stared dumbly at the indistinct photograph. He would never have known her. He let the paper slip through his trembling fingers.

'Talk about coincidence . . .' he muttered drily, reaching

for his whisky glass for support. 'It's like a Shakespearian comedy . . .'

He finished his drink. An inch of his cigarette remained; he sucked it down with one long thoughtful draw. His eyes narrowed. He looked at his watch.

'What's the time? Too late . . . Late, what's late? This is destiny. A tide in the affairs of men. Who can control his fate? To hell with the time . . .'

He leant across to the nearest bookshelf and pulled down his copy of *Contacts*. He skimmed through to the theatre addresses and found the number he wanted. He reached for the phone and dialled.

'Hello? Is that the Riverside? This is Philip Fletcher. I wonder – could you tell me how I can get hold of Sergei Shustikov?'

# 4

It is not considered usual in the theatrical world for the press to attend the first day of a rehearsal. Philip Fletcher was therefore a little surprised to be greeted on his arrival at the Riverside Studios by a bespectacled young woman of earnest appearance who proceeded to wave a microphone under his nose.

'Melissa Pine, Radio 4,' she said confidently.

Philip hesitated. From her tone of voice he inferred that this should have meant something to him, but it did not. He smiled sweetly though, for despite her unmistakable air of humourlessness she was quite an attractive young woman, while he was an extremely lecherous middle-aged man.

'I very much want to get the authentic background feel to rehearsals,' Melissa Pine went on, while Philip was thinking that he'd quite like to get the authentic background feel to her. 'It's very important to get an up-front in-depth interview for the programme with you, Philip.'

'Ah yes . . .'

He did now recall his agent saying something about the BBC doing some kind of Arts feature on the production, but he hadn't really taken it in. He frowned suspiciously.

'I'm sorry, isn't this a good time for you?' she asked, looking a little taken aback, as media people generally do when the possibility of an independent existence outside their orbit is even tentatively mooted.

'Oh, um, yes . . .' replied Philip, who was frowning only because he was thinking of his agent. 'Well, yes and no actually. I just want to see if there are any calls for me. Can we talk later?'

'Sure.' Melissa Pine reluctantly lowered her microphone. 'I'll be getting a coffee.'

'What a wonderful idea. Why don't you get me one and I'll come and find you.'

Philip went on through to reception to see if there were any messages. There was one. He carried the scrip of paper he had been given over to the payphones opposite.

'It's Philip Fletcher returning Howard Suter's call,' he said to the girl who answered. After a few moments he was transferred.

'Philip. Hi!' said a young American voice warmly.

'Howard?' Philip's tone was more uncertain. They had never met, but as complete strangers kept addressing him familiarly, he supposed it was the done thing to respond in kind.

'Sure is. Great to hear from you. I'm an admirer.'

'Thank you. You obviously got my letter.'

'Sure did. So, you're looking for representation. May I ask why?'

'Well, you know how it goes. No disrespect to John Quennell, but my career's not really advancing as it ought to, and perhaps our relationship's a little on the stale side. A change is as good as a rest, as they say.'

'Sure. Would you like to fix an appointment to come in and see me next week?'

'I'm on a tight rehearsal schedule at the moment – could we make it the week after?'

'I'll be in New York then, LA after that. Let's see – how about the twenty-third next month?'

'That's the day we open. Fine, it'll take my mind off it.'

'Great. What time's good for you?'

'Shall we say midday? Give me a chance to get over the dress rehearsal. Shall I come to your office?'

'Fine by me. Look forward to meeting you.'

Philip replaced the receiver with a flourish. Howard Suter was reputed to be the hottest young agent in London, and he had responded to his advances keenly. He tripped on through into the foyer feeling like a cat which has just won a weekend break to a dairy.

'Well now, look who's here!' said a fruity, familiar voice, as he approached the gaggle of actors congregating in the cafeteria. 'Our hope and our salvation. *Voilà l'homme!*'

Philip bowed discreetly.

'Why thank you, Seymour . . . I like the shirt: my compliments to the chef.'

Seymour Loseby idly folded his tomato-ketchup sleeves.

'That's the last time I give you an intro, duckie. Do you know everyone?'

Philip shook his head. Seymour introduced the actors playing Mardian and Agrippa and Philo/First Soldier. He was rather more interested in a strikingly pretty girl called Sally, who would be giving her Charmian. He offered her his most charming smile, but before he could switch on his auto-pilot proto-seductive patter, he noticed that Melissa Pine was waving to him from the other side of the room.

'It seems like I'm in demand, pray excuse me.'

Seymour laid a hand on his shoulder.

'Be warned, she's hard work.'

'I guessed as much.'

'Oh, and keep your fly buttons well done up. They don't call her Stripped Pine for nothing.'

Philip went on over, smiling sweetly.

'I didn't know if you wanted milk,' said Melissa, offering him a plastic carton.

'Fine as it is, thanks.'

As he sat down Philip tried to put the cup of coffee to his lips, but Melissa had put her microphone there first.

'Can you give me a level?' she asked, examining the dial on her recorder.

'I thought everyone who worked for the BBC had been sacked?'

'Not everyone. That's fine.'

She cleared her throat, pushed a stray length of brunette fringe back from her glasses, then thrust the microphone like Liberty's torch into the space between them.

'The Riverside Studios, London, Monday morning, late February,' she announced, in the kind of excited tone usually reserved in the contemporary media for weather forecasters. 'It's the first day of rehearsal and the actors are assembling in the cafeteria outside the auditorium. The atmosphere is tense and electric.'

Philip put a hand over his mouth to cover the first yawn of the morning.

'With me is Philip Fletcher, former member of the Royal Shakespeare Company and the Royal National Theatre Company, who will be playing Antony in the forthcoming production. Philip, will you tell me exactly what you're feeling now?'

'I'm feeling terribly excited and not a little nervous,' he lied smoothly. Actually he was feeling vaguely tired and specifically dyspeptic, but he didn't suppose that either she or her listeners would want to hear that. He was an old hand at supplying interviewers with exactly the kind of crap they did want to hear. Melissa seemed well satisfied by his answer.

'Could you tell us something about the dramatic turn of events which led to you being offered the part of Antony at the last minute?'

'Well, I think "dramatic" is overstating it somewhat. As you know, Ian had to pull out and I just happened to be in the right place at the right time.'

'And how do you feel about working with Sergei Shustikov?'

'Excited, naturally. He is one of the outstanding talents of world theatre and I've always wanted to work with him.'

'He has a reputation for being a very tough director. How do you think you'll handle that?'

'Oh, a lot of directors have that reputation. When I was younger I was terrified of John Dexter, but I survived. I think if you've lived through a tongue-lashing from John you can probably put up with anything.'

'How exactly did you come to be cast as Antony?'

'As I say, it was just chance. I happened to hear about Ian leaving the company, and as I've always been so desperate to work with Sergei I just leapt at the chance!'

'So did the approach come from you?'

'Yes. Yes, I was presumptuous enough to put my own name forward.'

'But he knew all about you, of course?'

'I believe I have a certain reputation, yes.'

'And the audition obviously went well.'

'It was a discussion rather than an audition. He seemed reasonably keen on me, yes.'

'But do you think there's a sense in which your casting could be construed as an act of desperation?'

'I hope you're not implying he was scraping the bottom of the barrel.'

'No, but how do you feel about not being first choice for the part?'

'Ian's loss, my gain, I think.'

'No, but after Ian dropped out he did offer the part to a number of other actors, didn't he?'

'Did he now? Well then, what a lucky little chap I am . . .'

Suddenly Melissa Pine snapped off the tape recorder and jumped up. Although Philip's answers had been steadily clouding with irritation, he was a little surprised at her abrupt reaction. Her attention, however, was no longer focused on him.

'Excuse me!' she said breathlessly, her face flushed with excitement. 'We'll have to finish another time. He's arrived!'

Even before he turned to face the door there was no doubt in Philip's mind who 'he' could be. All chatter had stopped; a devotional silence reigned. The pattering of Melissa's feet as she scurried towards the door, and the man in fur hat and coat who framed it, was the only sound.

'Sergei!'

Melissa waved her egregious microphone under the wide Tartarish nostrils.

'First day of rehearsals – how do you feel?'

The nostrils flared; a frown of disdain knitted the thickset eyebrows together.

'How I feel?' he growled in his pure Russian bass. 'You want to know how I feel? I tell you. Feel shit terrible!

Shit awful! Christ, this shit country! I want coffee. Get me!'

And so saying he stomped off heavily towards the auditorium, scowling like a bear roused prematurely from hibernation.

'Er, I think we'd better go on through, everyone,' said a young man wearing stage management battledress: roll-up cigarette; check shirt; bunch of keys, dangling from the hip for the use of. 'It's getting on for ten.'

Seymour Loseby came and slipped his arm through Philip's.

'Please sit next to me,' he said with affected nervousness. 'I'm going to need a big strong man on hand to protect me.'

'That's all very well,' Philip murmured, 'but who's going to protect me?'

Seymour laughed. 'Shall we go in?'

'I just want to . . . say hello. You go ahead, I'll come in a moment.'

'As the bishop said to the actress. My darling boy! How are you?' Seymour was off, in a cloud of dubious aftershave, flinging his arms round a pale young actor who seemed less than welcoming of his attentions. Philip hung back by the door, nodding and smiling to the others as they filed in ahead of him. At last only one remained.

'Hello, Natasha.'

She stopped abruptly. Her thoughts must have been elsewhere. It seemed that he had startled her, but he couldn't be sure: dark glasses covered her eyes.

'Why . . . Philip.'

The voice sounded a little wan, but the tone, like ten-year malt, was as rich as ever.

'You're looking well,' he said.

He wasn't sure that she did. He couldn't see the eyes behind the glasses, but he sensed anxiety, a touch of haggardness perhaps. What would she be now? Thirty-seven, thirty-eight? Perhaps a little fuller in the figure than he remembered, but why quibble? She was still drop-dead gorgeous.

'You too, Philip.'

She took his hand and squeezed it lightly. It was a distracted gesture, even as she made it she was craning her neck to peer past him into the auditorium. The lack of eye contact made him feel uneasy.

'I think we're wanted,' she said hurriedly.

As if on cue the deep booming voice of her lover came rumbling through the door:

'Natasha? Where the hell are you?'

She took a quick, nervous step towards the door. Just inside the light was poor, and she stopped for a moment to lift up her glasses. Philip caught a glimpse of a swollen red eye.

She dropped her glasses back into place and hurried on through. Philip followed, at a more measured pace.

'Where shit coffee?' the irascible director demanded as he made his entrance. 'Get me now!'

Philip walked slowly on to the stage towards the semicircle of chairs laid out in readiness for the read through.

'At least we know why they call him Shitski,' he murmured as he sat down next to Seymour. His old friend grunted.

'My dear, you ain't heard nothing yet . . .'

# 5

'Shit awful! Damn shit awful! Why you give me this bloody crap? You shit terrible actors, or what?'

Philip lowered his crossword for a moment and glanced at the actors lining the other end of the rehearsal room. They were wearing the kind of disorientated look one sees in wartime photographs of Blitz survivors.

'You loads of bloody useless shit!'

Useless shit? Philip wondered. Wherefore the useful variety? His hand hovered uncertainly over three across.

'You damn crap lot!'

Philip sighed and put down his paper. It was hard trying to concentrate, even when the answer to the clue was on the tip of his brain. 'Much sport makes three-time lunatic' (seven letters). Shakespeare, of course, but which one? Or, as one distinguished Slavonic interpreter might have said – which shit Shakespeare?

It had not been so on their first meeting; at least, not initially.

'Philip! Delighted to meet you! I am great fan!'

'Me too – I mean, I'm a fan of yours.'

Philip had laughed nervously. Which production could he pretend he'd seen? Fortunately he was saved from spurious invention.

'I tell you about production,' said Shustikov without preamble, leaning across the table in his office and becoming animated. Philip instinctively recoiled, and not just from the wave of blue Gauloise smoke which the Russian breathed into his face. Although not a large man (he was about Philip's height and build), Shustikov had a big coarse presence. A thick mane of grey-black hair and an unruly beard gave him a grizzled, earthy air. He banged on the table for emphasis with a meaty, dirty-nailed fist.

'I tell you about *Antony and Cleopatra*. Is passionate play.'

'Yes.'

'But is middle-age passion. Is not *Romeo and Juliet* sort of shit.'

'No?'

'No. Is different kind of shit entirely. Is important difference.'

'You mean the shit's relative?'

'Damn right. She gypsy. He Rome. He soldier, cold imperial power. She is light, Mediterranean, sun.'

'Rome's quite sunny from time to time, isn't it?'

'Not desert heat. I talk about red-hot Egyptian shit. You know what I mean?'

'Mm . . .'

'Good. We see eye to eye. I like.'

Philip wasn't exactly sure that they did, but he was prepared to feign accord. Bizarre as Shustikov sounded, the Russian had one fundamental quality which excused all demerits as far as Philip was concerned – the quality of not being Ben Ferris.

'You bloody shit useless idiots!'

On the other hand, he wasn't Tyrone Guthrie either.

Philip put the cap back on his biro and laid it down neatly next to his folded newspaper. At the other end of the room Shustikov was yelling at the pitiful few who, under the rigours of theatrical economy, were attempting to impersonate the full splendours of the Egyptian court.

'And you worse damn actress of all!'

He was standing over Natasha, who was on the floor in the midst of an assortment of cushions. He towered above her with legs arrogantly spread and arms akimbo; a tyrant bestriding his narrow world.

Natasha's eyes glistened with hurt. Hers was a classic peaches and cream complexion, but today her cheeks were rather more fruit than dairy. She did not look happy.

'Sergei,' she said quietly. 'We're doing our best.'

'Best? This worse bloody shit I ever saw!'

Worse even than yesterday's? Philip wondered; or the day's before? It was only the third day of rehearsal, but it was hard to see how much deeper into the critical cesspool they could all sink. All of them except Philip.

'This damn shit-hot good actor!' Shustikov had roared publicly in his ear yesterday, finding time to slap him across the shoulders in between aiming sharp jabs below the belt at everyone else.

Possibly for the first time in his life Philip had found praise discomfiting. It wasn't that he considered it unmerited, but that Shustikov was using it as a means to browbeat his peers. Philip had often been in companies where the director had singled out one actor as his whipping boy. What was unusual in this instance was that he seemed to have selected the rest of the cast.

Philip didn't know why he had been so singularly honoured, but he didn't like it. He had enough problems on his plate already without having to cope with the resentment of his co-mates and sisters in Equity. Even Seymour was affording him a wary eye.

'Take top of bloody scene again,' Shustikov rasped.

The Russian turned away with a disgusted look. He caught Philip's eye and gave him a snarl of a smile implicit with shared disdain. Philip looked down hurriedly and scrutinized three across.

He had met some bullies in his time, but Shitski was the worst – the reality, if anything, exceeded the reputation. He would start ranting and yelling without warning, but it was hard to discern what point he was making. But if he seemed to have difficulty communicating, considerations of language were probably secondary: Philip was convinced that he wouldn't have made any more sense in Russian. He was surly, sarcastic, scornful, and that was on a good day; in a bad mood he was shit horrible.

'Charmian,' said Natasha, beginning the scene again.

'Madam.'

'Ha, ha! Give me to drink mandragora—'

41

'Shit what you drink?'

Philip sighed as he looked at his watch. Three days in and they were still crawling through the blocking of Act I. There were two more scenes to go before he would be needed again, and many of the actors sitting around him had not yet been used at all.

'I'm sorry, Sergei.' said Natasha quietly.

Philip kept his eyes down. He didn't want to look at Natasha; having to listen to the humiliation in her voice was bad enough.

'Sorry, ha!' her lover guffawed nastily. 'What you think you say? You not in shit bar now, you know, not in bloody pub for Christ sake, ask for shit gin and tonic, shit cube of ice and shit lemon! What is you say?'

Philip noticed Melissa Pine in the corner, her microphone thrust forward and an expression of intense concentration on her face. What was she going to do with all her tapes? Philip asked himself. At this rate she wasn't going to get two consecutive sentences fit to broadcast.

'Charmian.'

'Madam!'

'Ha, ha! Give me to drink mandragora—'

'Damn crap!' the director interjected violently, kicking a nearby chair for emphasis. Natasha froze.

'What you say in scene?' Shitski demanded, barging over and glowering down at her once more. 'Is drink you want? Like hell! Is Antony you want. You want red-hot shit-hot sex, no? Not damn drink, dammit! If Antony come now he want to screw you? Nah!'

The Russian turned away scornfully. His eyes lit on Sally, who was standing behind Natasha. He pointed a stubby finger at her: 'Now *that* I want to screw!' he declared salaciously. Sally and Natasha both blushed violently. Shitski savoured their discomfort.

'Where is sex appeal?' he demanded, returning to attack Natasha once again. 'Why should Antony sacrifice world for you? He come back now he have handmaiden, not Cleopatra, he have any damn sense at all. You look like pile of shit sitting there. What man in right mind would want to screw you, huh?'

'I would,' said Philip.

Shitski rounded furiously on the voice, but when he saw that it was his leading actor who had spoken, his anger turned to surprise. Philip ignored him. He kept his eyes on Natasha, whose cheeks were only a little less red than previously. He thought he detected the ghost of a smile on her lips.

'Yah! I can't take no more of this damn shit!' scowled her lover. 'Have break. Have tea. Bloody English drink shit tea. Next do act two. Get me coffee. Now.'

Philip slipped out discreetly and made his way downstairs to the cafeteria. In the queue he met Sally and Vicki, the actress playing Iras.

'Mind if I sit with you?' he asked pleasantly as they collected their coffees.

'Um, we're not stopping actually,' said Sally.

Vicki laughed nervously. 'We think we'd better go straight back up; daren't be late!'

Philip carried his cup over to a table and sat down alone. At least he had his crossword with him. He unfolded the paper and stared at the recalcitrant clue.

'Much sport makes three-time lunatic . . .'

He wasn't in the best of spirits. There was a bitter residue in his mouth and it wasn't on account of the low-grade coffee, which tasted suspiciously like Ebony Smooth. He jabbed forcefully at the paper with his biro, improvising an abstract pointillist doodle.

'Much sport? ... That's *Lear*, Gloucester on Edmund: "Much sport in his making". Lunatic? What's that? Bugger. Damn, bugger and blast, it's no good . . .'

He dropped his pen on to the table. What was he doing here? What did he think he was up to? Getting involved had seemed like his destiny; turning the tables on fate. No sulking at his snub from Ferris, he'd just gone straight out and found the perfect vehicle to prove his point. It had all been so easy: when Shustikov returned his call he'd been practically heavy breathing down the line. And no wonder, if what Melissa Pine had implied was true – that every other leading actor in London had turned him down. Would he have even tried for the part in different circumstances? Probably not, given Shitski's reputation. He certainly wasn't doing it for the money. Why was he doing it then? There was the little matter of the leading actress.

'Philip? May I join you?'

He started. He had been so locked in himself he hadn't seen her come up. He gave an embarrassed smile.

'Of course, Natasha. Actually, I was just thinking about you . . .'

She smiled back and a little knot tightened within him. Had he been merely infatuated with her all those years ago, or had it been love? Knowing himself, the former was more likely, though his natural cynicism had been in some measure of abeyance then. These days, of course, it was rampant.

'Nothing bad I hope . . . Thank you for speaking up for me in rehearsal.'

It was Philip's turn to blush. He felt himself begin to melt in her big brown eyes. He looked down.

'I'm sorry about Sergei,' she went on. 'He can be a bit awkward sometimes.'

'Oh, yes,' answered Philip hesitantly, slightly shocked at the enormity of her understatement. And why was she apologizing to him anyway? She was his principal victim.

'I know he's difficult,' she continued, 'but I'm afraid geniuses are just like that, you have to make allowances.'

Philip wondered how long it would be before Shustikov's genius began manifesting itself. He had a dark suspicion that it might be like waiting for the return of Captain Oates.

'Where did you two meet?' he asked, steering the conversation into the safe waters of harmless small talk.

'In Los Angeles. The Festival. Hedda Gabler. I was over there doing a small part in a film, someone suggested me to him. I was lucky, on the spot.'

'And you've been in the States since then?'

'The last eighteen months, yes. Not working much, though.'

'Visa problems?'

44

'No, no, I've got the green card. It's just that Sergei's very restless, he's always on the move. It's not easy to find parts if you haven't got a base.'

'Yes, I can see that.'

Philip wondered just how much Shustikov's wanderlust was self-decreed. He couldn't imagine that there were many theatres – still fewer actors – prepared to put up with him twice.

'He's a very sweet man really,' Natasha was saying. 'It's just that he's so passionate about the theatre he gets carried away sometimes.'

There was a touch of anxiety in her voice, the hint of a desperate need to be believed. When she spoke of him there was almost an echo of religious fervour. Philip guessed that she was willing herself to believe it too.

'I was thinking about Bristol today,' he said. 'Remember that club we used to go to, opposite the theatre?'

'Go to?' She laughed. 'We practically lived there!'

'Yes . . .' He laughed too, though more out of relief than pleasure: it was the first hint of merriment he'd seen in her.

'That was a great season, wasn't it?'

Her voice was wistful, her smile faint and far away. He kept silent while she remembered. He was remembering himself. He felt uncomfortable.

'Yes,' she repeated at last. 'We had a lot of fun, didn't we?'

*Fun*. She paused before saying the word, parenthesizing it, pushing it to arm's length. So much the classical actress, the poignancy of her phrasing disturbed him; it was like hearing Electra mourn Iphigenia. He remembered her on stage at the Bristol Old Vic, binding the audience to their seats with the wounded charge in her voice.

He found he couldn't look at her. He was unused to dealing with emotions, his or anyone else's. What was this fun she remembered having? His own recollections had a different colour. Was she trying to fool him, or just herself? He didn't have a clue. He felt as mixed up as she was. She was almost an item of his mental furniture, she had been there so long, yet he hardly knew her. She was an intimate stranger. He didn't know how to handle this situation. The silence was becoming awkward, he had no idea what to say. He didn't begin to understand her relationship with Shitski. It was none of his business, he shouldn't get drawn in. Why did she let him treat her like that?

'Ooh, aren't you a little darling!' she said suddenly.

For a moment Philip was understandably surprised, but then he realized that she was addressing not him but a small child sitting on her mother's lap at the next table.

'Aah! Isn't she adorable, Philip?'

Philip turned awkwardly in his seat to look at the pudgy pink bundle in a romper suit. The featureless rubbery face was unevenly daubed with ice-cream and snot.

'Delightful,' he remarked politely.

'Ooh, what a sweetie!' said Natasha, making a tickling mime with her fingers. Philip, mildly embarrassed, looked down at his paper.

'Care for another coffee?' he asked casually, attempting to ignore her regression into babytalk. He considered the irritating crossword clue for a moment before glancing up again.

'Good God!' he exclaimed, shocked. 'Are you all right?'

Tears were streaming down her face. She looked completely distraught.

'I'd better go,' she gasped, stifling a sob in a hastily snatched tissue. 'We'll be starting again in a minute . . .'

Before he could say anything she leapt up and ran off to the stairs, crashing blindly into chairs and tables as she went.

'Oh no . . .' Philip murmured disconsolately.

His heart was sinking fast. He watched her as she turned the corner, her shoulders anxiously hunched, her wet cheek pale with nerves. She looked on the verge of a breakdown. There were four and a half weeks of rehearsal to go; how was she going to cope? What had Shitski done to her?

'By God, he must have knocked it out of you!'

He'd encountered that loss of confidence in many actors, he'd been as near as dammit at the nadir himself, but it seemed to him as if Natasha had had it beaten out of her systematically.

She was more like a battered housewife than the vibrant young actress he had once idolized. That Shitski had a lot to answer for.

'What a bastard . . .'

Philip snatched up his paper. That was it – of course! Three across, seven letters: much sport in whose making? Edmund's. Three-time lunatic? 'Mad kings, mad world, mad composition.' King John, the Bastard's speech. Edmund the bastard. B-A-S-T-A-R-D.

'Ha!'

Philip scribbled in the seven letters and threw down the completed crossword triumphantly. At least Shustikov had been good for something.

# 6

Shitski hadn't been the first bastard in Natasha's life, not by a long chalk. There had been Bristol.

Philip had been so excited about that season. It had taken a tough audition and two recalls to get into the Old Vic company, in those days one of the best reps in the country. He'd been offered a decent run of parts too: Solyony in *Three Sisters*, Lodovico in *The White Devil*, plus a bit of light relief in the Panto. At the time the Bristol Old Vic was one of the few regional theatres which had not had to resort to Christmas productions of *Joseph and the Amazing Technicolor Dreamcoat* in order to keep afloat. For that Philip had been profoundly grateful.

He had been less happy about his digs, a peeling damp basement in the bowels of a Gothic monstrosity at the Downs end of Pembroke Road. At least the landlady, a semi-deaf kindly old soul, was little in evidence after she'd offered the daily plateful of fried grease optimistically advertised as breakfast. For a time Philip had thought there might be other compensations as well.

The first person he saw at the read through was also the only one in the company he knew, Dick Jones. His feelings towards Jones had been neutral then. They had exchanged small talk, in the course of which Philip was pleased to discover that he had been offered much the better parts. In *Three Sisters*, the first production, Jones had been cast as one of the artillery officers, an unnamed bit part. Even that, Philip was later to muse, put a severe strain on his abilities.

'I've got great digs,' Jones had confided, anxious to make a minor claim of his own in the oneupmanship stakes. This would be a recurring feature in their future relationship.

'It's this big house up in Redland, full of students. And talk about nubile ... you won't see better crumpet in a bakery, boyo!'

Philip was already beginning to decide that he didn't much care for Dick Jones. His heavily emphasized Welshness was one good reason (the professional Celt vying only with the professional Northerner for first place in the Theatrical Bores stakes), his crude salaciousness another. Philip just wasn't comfortable with sex. He was certainly interested in it, perhaps even obsessed, but he wasn't good at it. His affairs were usually brief and unsatisfactory. Although he would not have admitted as much, he was seriously repressed.

So he was jealous of people who weren't, people like Dick Jones. Jones was openly lecherous, he exuded confidence and self-belief. He knew how to get women into bed, or at least he implied he did. Philip could only pretend that he was in on the secret too.

'Bet she goes like a rocket,' Jones had murmured into his ear when the first of the actresses arrived. When a female ASM appeared he nudged Philip hard in the ribs: 'That's a goer if ever I saw one, you can always tell by ... Christ! Who's that?'

The awestruck tone in his voice made Philip turn. The girl who had just come in must have known they were talking about her. Probably every man in the room was, but Philip was the one she noticed staring. He blushed.

'Bloody hell!' whispered Dick Jones. 'What a stunner!'

Stunned was just how Philip felt. He couldn't take his eyes off her. When they assembled for the read through he chose a chair opposite so that he could peer at her surreptitiously over the top of his text. And when she was introduced by the director and he heard the part that she was playing his heart fluttered: she was Irina, the youngest sister, and the object of his, Solyony's, unrequited desire. He was actually meant to stare at her. For the first time in his life he willingly embraced the precepts of the Method actor.

All morning he had eyes and ears only for her. It dimly occurred to him that he ought to stop himself, to get a grip, that a schoolboy crush was an unseemly thing for a man turned thirty to bear, but mere awareness of the affliction was not enough to effect a cure. Infatuation was in his nature, it was a corollary of his underdeveloped emotions. Had he not for the last ten years been hopelessly in thrall to Hannah Sheridan, a gorgeous gaudy butterfly as far removed from his grasp as the planets? Looking back on his youth from the dubious haven of middle age Philip was never less than appalled to recall the extent of his own gaucheness and ineffectuality. He had gone through his early life like a midget through a fancy goods shop, attracted only to the inaccessible top shelves.

Natasha had something of Hannah about her, no doubt it partly explained Philip's interest. They had the same dark-haired, pale-skinned look, though Natasha's face was more chiselled and her figure leaner and longer. She lacked Hannah's physical voluptuousness, but there was the same figurative promise in her eyes – almond-brown, to Hannah's deep-sea green. Both possessed a fleshly vitality which Philip, in all his plastic orthodoxy, found exotic and irresistible.

But at least he was used to Hannah. Natasha ambushed him, and the surprise was total. She was also a much better actress than Hannah, he realized that as soon as she opened her mouth. Her face looked too young for her voice, which had the resonance and clarity to bounce back effortlessly from the farthest gallery. All her acting skills betokened a maturity beyond her years. He listened admiringly to her perfect phrasing and exquisite modulation. This Irina would break the audience's hearts.

He hadn't been prescient enough to discern that she might break his own. He was naive, sometimes, to the point of imbecility. He had the wit of a rabbit staring into the oncoming headlamps.

Much later he came to understand all this. His twenties and thirties – his so-called youth – were an insipid featureless stretch of time, in which the blandness of his personality found an echo in his solid dull career. During those years sourness brewed within him, eroding his mind and spirit. It had taken a bizarre accident of fate, his own unique brand of Macbeth-like shock aversion therapy, to salvage his work, and thus his life. It was not overstating the case dramatically to put it in those terms. In the event he had even caught, however briefly, that butterfly Hannah, his tormenting siren. He had learnt that in order to reach the top shelf, he had only to stand on a ladder.

But that priceless knowledge lay a long time ahead of him during the Bristol season. Unfleshed as his own character was, he was only really happy expressing himself through his acting. His clamped desires concentrated his energies inwards and his work on the Old Vic stage that autumn was to be more powerful and focused than anything he had ever done. He picked up some of the best reviews of his career, but his circle of admirers extended beyond the ranks of the critics. Natasha Fielding was at its epicentre.

The discovery of her regard for him acted like a drug on his confidence. They had hardly spoken during the month of rehearsals, even though he did the bulk of his scenes with her. Luckily she told him.

The day before the dress rehearsal he got on the bus to go home and there she was, just ahead of him in the queue. Her smile froze him with terror, but he would have to join her, it would have looked odd not to. Philip had a rooted paranoia about looking odd.

'I didn't know you went this way,' he said as he sat next to her.

'I didn't. I've just moved.'

'To Clifton?'

'Pembroke Road.'

She'd been staying with a friend the past month on the other side of town, she told him. The friend had said she could stay, but she wanted to move out to Clifton. She had lived there during her time at the drama school, which she had left only the summer before last. It was by far the prettiest part of Bristol.

'I couldn't wait to get back there,' she told him eagerly. 'Though my friend's been awfully sweet.'

'I bet he's sorry to see you go.'

'It's a girl friend actually . . . I think she's probably relieved to see the back of me!'

Philip laughed along with her. He was relieved that it had not been a male friend. He thought he had fished for that one pretty well.

'Are you living alone in your new place?' he asked, fishing more boldly.

'Yes. You know what I look forward to seeing again most in Clifton?'

He shook his head. She laughed again.

'I know it sounds silly . . . but I really want to see the zoo. I can't wait. We had this wonderful teacher at the school, he told us to study the animals and learn about characters. It's amazing, but I'll swear there's a gorilla in there that's the spitting image of Falstaff!'

He wondered if there was anything in the reptile house that looked like Dick Jones.

'Sounds fascinating,' he said politely, though he didn't really mean it.

'Not that you'd need to go there, of course,' she added hastily, perhaps alerted by the insincerity of his tone. 'I haven't had a chance to tell you – well, I know we've hardly spoken – but I really do think your performance is brilliant. No, honestly, I mean it . . .'

She had to repeat herself, because he was so practised in self-effacement that a spluttered denial erupted instantly from his lips. She would have none of it.

'It's a wonderful performance, really it is. I didn't know the play before, and to be honest when I read it through I didn't even notice your part. You've brought it to life. And when I saw you at the technical rehearsal – well, I couldn't believe it! I don't know what you did with your make-up, your hair, but you just didn't look like you any more. That really was Solyony standing there on stage with me. I felt a little tingling in my spine!'

From anyone else Philip would have considered the compliment no more than well-merited (self-effacement was only a motion), but coming from her it swelled and emboldened him.

And though a supreme rationalist, the discovery that henceforth she would be living a few doors down from him nurtured a superstitious inkling that fate might be giving him a nudge.

'I'd like to see that gorilla at the zoo,' he told her, when they had both got off at the same bus stop and were about to go their separate ways.

'I'd love to show him to you,' Natasha answered. 'Why don't we go on Sunday?'

The suggestion had come from her. He thought about it, over and over again, as he lay in bed that night unable and unwilling to sleep. It had been her idea that they spend their only free day of the week together. It was just a visit to Bristol Zoo, not a candlelit dinner for two in an aphrodisiac Caribbean hideaway, but such fine distinctions were lost on Philip. His imagination grew as ripe as Malvolio's.

There was the little matter of the rest of the week to get through first, a week that included not just an opening night but the first rehearsals for the next production. It would have been nice to have had a break between the two, but the necessities of theatrical economy permitted no slackening. Thursday at eleven was the time assigned for the read through of *The White Devil*, the morning after the first performance of *Three Sisters*.

Philip arrived for it in an agitated state. The company had all gone out to a restaurant to celebrate after last night's opening. He had shadowed Natasha closely, but at the crucial moment he was distracted and Dick Jones sidled in beside her. Philip was forced to sit at the next table. Wine flowed, everyone was in the best of spirits; everyone except Philip. He watched Dick Jones's transparent manoeuvrings with concentrated loathing. Although the evening ended with Natasha sharing Philip's cab back to Clifton, he was cool and kept his distance. She had laughed much too uproariously at Jones's unfunny jokes.

The green-eyed monster was Philip's familiar. He came and sat on his shoulder the next morning. His tenure had nothing to do with Dick Jones.

They had a new director for *The White Devil*. Julian Carne

was young, intense and ruthlessly ambitious. He had an eye for talent, and an eye for a pretty girl. Both of them focused on Natasha.

Where and how he did his work Philip was too unskilled to notice, but even by Sunday the first trenches had been dug and the sieging batteries emplaced. The plan had been for Philip to knock on Natasha's door at two and walk her to the zoo, but it had to be changed.

'Could we make it three tomorrow?' she asked him as they got out of their shared cab on Saturday night. 'Julian's taking me to lunch. I'll come and get you.'

In the event she turned up at ten to four.

'We'd better hurry,' she said after she had apologized. 'It'll be closing soon.'

It was a gloomy winter afternoon, the better to match Philip's mood. It did not improve when he got out on to the pavement and saw that Julian was waiting in his car.

'He asked if he could come too,' Natasha explained casually. 'I said I was sure you wouldn't mind.'

Julian's car was a bright red MG. Philip had to squeeze into the luggage area in the back. Natasha stretched out her long slim legs in front.

'It's not far,' said the director dismissively, slipping off the handbrake and brushing Natasha's thigh with the back of his hand. She was in alcoholic high spirits, and she either didn't notice or didn't mind. Philip seethed helplessly.

'It's a bit late,' commented Julian, slowing but not stopping outside the zoo. 'It closes at five, doesn't it?'

'Half past, I think,' said Philip.

'Either way there's not really enough time. Let's get a drink.'

'I want to go to the zoo,' said Philip stubbornly, though he couldn't have cared less about the sodding zoo.

'Then you'd better get out,' replied Julian coolly. 'Natasha, let him out . . .'

She turned round in her seat. She gave him a bland smile.

'Julian's right,' she said. 'It is late. Do you really want to go?'

'Let him if he wants to,' Julian muttered. There was an edge in his voice.

'It's too early to get a drink,' Philip protested sulkily.

'Don't be a wet blanket!' scoffed Julian. 'Go on, get out if you're going.'

Philip looked pleadingly at Natasha. He got only the cosmetic smile in response.

'Perhaps I would like a drink after all,' he mumbled.

Julian Carne didn't look pleased. He put his car into gear with another unnecessary knee-stroke and thrust his foot down aggressively. Philip clung on in a costive hunch behind him.

They drove over to Redland. Julian was staying in the same house as Dick Jones and some of the other actors. Dick was there when they went in, watching the television in a communal living room that resembled a waste tip. Julian invited him to join them in a bottle of wine.

Two more actors turned up, a second bottle was cracked open, then a third. Dick Jones turned off the TV and put on a record, some thin-voiced pop singer they all seemed to know except Philip. He sat in silence while they sang along, sipping the sour unpleasant wine. He hated them all, except Natasha, whom he hated and loved at once.

She sat between Dick and Julian, the lone female, the natural centre of attention. She'd already been drinking, the wine made her glow. Philip sat morosely in the corner, out of her radiance. He did not contribute to the conversation, which was rapid and light and made the others laugh, though the next day he couldn't remember a word of it. He might just as well not have been there. He should have left. He wanted to go, but he was too weak. He stayed and wallowed in humiliation and misery. The afternoon dragged on and on.

When seven o'clock came Julian suggested going to the pub. The response was lukewarm. Philip kept quiet in the corner and listened to the others dithering. After a minute of inert discussion he got to his feet and went upstairs to find the bathroom. When he came back down again, Julian and Natasha had gone.

'Took her home, I think,' said Dick Jones when he asked where they'd gone. Jones gave a dirty chuckle. 'Lucky bastard . . .'

He walked back to Clifton through the cold and drizzly night. It had been a pleasant afternoon when he'd come out, he was wearing only a thin jacket. He walked fast and almost didn't notice the freezing air. The house in Pembroke Road where she lived was dark and obviously empty, as he had known it would be. Darkness, dampness and coldness enveloped him in a fallacious fog of pathos. He went home and stared at the clock. Later, wearing a thick coat, he came out again, but the house was still gloomy. She had still not returned by two the next morning, when he at last went to bed. As he walked down to the bus stop the next morning he noticed that her curtains were still exactly half-drawn, as they had been the previous evening.

Philip focused his energies still more into his work and concentrated on getting through the rest of the miserable season. It wasn't easy enduring rehearsals, watching Julian direct Natasha, seeing how by manner and gesture he implied his easy possession of her. She was playing the lead, Vittoria Corombona, a big break for a young actress, and she was nervous. He treated her casually, almost with brusqueness, even in the breaks between rehearsals. It was as if, having secured her, he began immediately to lose interest. Natasha's confidence was affected. Sometimes, waiting at the bus stop in the morning, Philip would see them drive by in Julian's red MG. Usually she looked pale and tired. After a few weeks Philip moved to a much nicer flat off Whiteladies Road. He told everyone that he was tired of his damp basement.

The tense atmosphere which developed in rehearsal (and Philip was not alone in noticing it) was eased once the production opened and Julian went back to London, but his frequent return visits reimposed it instantly. Philip didn't speak much to Natasha, but backstage was a whispering gallery and he knew she was unhappy. Julian had another girlfriend in London, he heard. Julian had promised to give her up, but he hadn't. The other girl became pregnant, the rumour ran. As

*The White Devil* ended, Julian's appearances became less frequent.

Only the panto remained for Philip. The Artistic Director had spoken about extending his contract, but he had declined. He needed the work, but he needed to be away from Bristol more. Natasha was staying on for the rest of the season.

He got on with his job. He even found a girlfriend, temporarily, till Dick Jones took her away from him. On his last night in Bristol, the Saturday of the final performance, there was going to be a party at the house Dick Jones and the other two actors shared. Philip bumped into Natasha in the corridor as he left his dressing room.

'Coming to the party?' she asked.

'No.'

She looked surprised. 'Why not?'

'I've got a lot of packing.'

One suitcase and a holdall hardly constituted a lot. She didn't look as if she believed him.

'Parties aren't really my scene,' he added. 'I'm feeling tired.'

'Aren't we all!'

Panto schedules were always exhausting, due to the combination of screaming kids and multiple matinees, but that was hardly a convincing excuse either: it being the end of the run, everyone else was so high as to be almost delirious.

'I'm sorry you're not staying on,' she told him. 'Got a job to go to?'

'No.'

'I'm surprised you're leaving.'

'You sound like my agent.'

She laughed. He hadn't said it to be funny, his annoyance grew. Was it really possible she didn't know why he was going? He felt that she was playing with him.

'I'm sorry we never made it to the zoo,' she said pleasantly.

'Well don't look at me!' he snapped. 'Got to go . . .'

'Philip!' She sounded surprised and concerned. She extended her hand to him. 'Goodbye, then.'

His arms hung limply by his sides while an emotional storm raged within him. Should he take her hand, or should he just march off? That would be childish and petulant, how could he even think of behaving in that way? Yet that was exactly what he was thinking. What was she doing by offering her hand? Was it absurd politeness, a meaningless gesture, or an invitation to collusion? Let's pretend, was she implying, pretend that nothing ever happened, that feelings weren't trampled upon, that everything in the garden's rosy? Fie, 'tis an unweeded garden. That it should come to this! Frailty, thy name is woman! Or was it possible she didn't know? Could she be blind to his feelings? What about her own feelings? What was she doing with Julian Carne? What was she doing to herself? He was going, he might never see her again, why shouldn't he speak openly? He could see himself going out into the cold night, alone but unburdened, a true romantic hero. Her hand, what did that signify? He should seize her in his arms, like Caspar Goodwood in *The Portrait of a Lady*, sear her lips with passionate white lightning, then stride out like the noble literary hero he would have been such natural casting for, with her rushing after him, begging him not to go, saying, no, no, I was mistaken, I see it all now, Julian means nothing to me, a satyr to your Hyperion, please take me in your arms and save me from myself ... Yes, but what if they weren't reading from the same script? Isabel had just run off, she hadn't followed Caspar. He might end up looking an awful prat. Could he take the risk? Did he dare to eat a peach?

'Goodbye,' he said, and shook her hand, and left.

No, he was not Prince Troilus, nor Romeo, nor any swain of that ilk. He was Philip boring bloody Fletcher, a permanent fresher in the university of life; a name below the title; a byword for inadequacy. He was never going to amount to anything. What had he been doing, thinking a girl like that, a golden girl with the world at her feet, would ever see anything in a hopeless worthless ill-fated wretch like him? Where had he been keeping his brain all these weeks?

He went over it all in his head, again and again, in every painful humiliating detail, on the train back from Bristol. He could have gone on *Mastermind* – specialist subject: Self-pity. He sat locked in the toilet for most of the journey, staring at the top of his head in the juddering mirror, listening to the mood music in the monotonous hum of the rails, a perfect accompaniment to the single-tracked line of his thought. He argued with himself aloud, as he always did, always had done, his initially reasoned tone converting by degrees to ramble and rant as the bottle of Scotch he had purchased earlier came to be emptied. By the time they reached Paddington he was wildly drunk. He hadn't been used to alcohol in those days.

He thought at first that the uniformed men waiting for him when he emerged from the lavatory were there to help. He did not realize until much later that they were transport policemen and that they were there to arrest him on suspicion of travelling without a ticket. It did not aid his cause that in his inebriated state he was temporarily unable to locate the proof of his innocence.

'No!' Philip declared grandiosely, as the two policemen fell in on either side to pin his arms. 'I am not Prince Hamlet!'

The policemen seemed to imply from their looks that he should not have expected preferential treatment even had his identity as Royal Dane been confirmed. Their grip on his arms tightened.

No, not Troilus, not Romeo, and certainly not poor batty Hamlet. One day, though, he was going to be Antony. Had Madame Sosostris, the famous clairvoyant, happened to be on hand with her wicked pack of cards to tell him as much, he would have been very considerably surprised. And he would have been even more surprised to discover the identity of his Cleopatra.

# 7

Two old actors were once more propping up the backstage bar at the National Theatre.

'Crowded tonight,' remarked Seymour Loseby, handing over a replenished Guinness with raspberry top. His friend shrugged phlegmatically as he lifted the pint glass to his lips.

'First night, isn't it? Open season for freeloaders. Call me a cynic if you will.'

'I will: you're a cynic. What's the word?'

'What's the word on what?'

'What do you think? First night, you just said.'

'You mean our *Antony and Cleopatra*?'

'Well, I don't mean *The Mousetrap*, do I?'

'One can never be sure with you. I've heard it's good.'

'*Antony and Cleopatra*, you mean?'

'Of course that's what I mean. You don't think I'd call *The Mousetrap* good, do you, you camp old fool?'

'All right, keep your rug on. So Ben Ferris has done the business?'

'Apparently. They say Dick Jones is bloody good.'

'Philip'll be sick.'

'You mean my alleged lookalike?'

'The same.'

'How's yours going then?'

'Don't ask.'

'I just did.'

'Pretend you didn't.'

'I can't, I'm intrigued. How bad is it?'

'Very.'

'Can you be more specific?'

'Well, put it this way. Remember the Titanic?'

'I see. Hit a few icebergs, have we? Shitski living up to his name?'

'Living down to it, more like.'

'Well, you can't say I didn't warn you.'

'I won't, but I'm hardly in a position to pick and choose my employers these days, am I?'

'You mean no one else'll have you?'

'That's one way of putting it.'

'And when do you open?'

'Tomorrow.'

'Good God, I didn't realize it was so soon. Bit unfortunate you opening straight after the production here, isn't it?'

'We were meant to go a week earlier. Shitski apparently planned it that way, to pip your lot at the post. That was before Ian dropped out.'

'Don't call them my lot, I just work here.'

'Is the *Antony* in the Lyttleton?'

'Olivier. I saw ten minutes of a preview the other night.'

'And?'

'As I said, looks good.'

'Ours doesn't.'

'So you say.'

'Ours looks dreadful. Silliest set I ever saw.'

'Careful, I can think of a few contenders.'

'You won't match this. Shitski's set it in Murmansk.'

'What?'

'That's what it looks like anyway. The back of the set is a frozen wasteland, a kind of junkyard with scaffolding and an abandoned Ford Cortina stuck under a snowdrift in the middle.'

'Is the make of car significant?'

'I wouldn't like to say. Centre forestage there's a sandpit. That's where Cleopatra's court hangs out, only every time there's a Roman scene we're meant to kick a bit more snow into the middle, so that by the end she can build herself an igloo.'

'Doesn't it melt?'

'It's not real snow, you fool, it's some yucky polystyrene

muck. There's a bloodstained sheet hanging up at the back, too, just behind the Ford Cortina.'

'What for?'

'My dear, you know better than to ask questions like that. But we have to tear it down at the end and roll Philip in it.'

'What about cossies?'

'Romans wear pinstripe suits; Egyptians look like failed cabaret turns at the Folies-Bergère.'

'How bizarre. They've Balkanized it here you know. The Roman army all wear blue helmets like the UN.'

'I'd heard. No one's got the legs for togas any more.'

'True. Must be the modern diet. What's Shitski trying to say?'

'God knows. He muttered something about frozen capitalism and the revolution of the senses on the first day, but nothing since. He's not exactly a natural communicator. He's one of those directors who wouldn't deem it worth his intellectual while talking to mere actors anyway.'

'Dear heart, how bittersweet you are, and how well it becomes you! How's my lookalike coping with it all?'

'Badly. I almost feel sorry for him.'

'Only almost?'

'Shitski sucks up to him, talks down to the rest of us.'

'Typical. Did I not warn you that Shustikov was the Stalin of the footlights? Have I told you about when those Russians were here for the international theatre season a few years back? It was just after *perestroika*, we were all being very chummy. Can't remember how, but the subject of Shitski came up, and our stage manager, who'd been with him at the Edinburgh Festival the year he defected, said, "Actually you can have him back if you want." Bit of an awkward silence, as you might imagine, but then one of them said, "It's all right, thanks, you can keep him." I wonder if he's part of an old KGB plot to destabilize western culture.'

'If he is, he's succeeding. I know it's not Philip's fault if Shitski sucks up to him, but it's not much fun for the rest of us. Natasha's the one who's really suffering, mind. He treats her like dirt.'

'Philip does?'

'No, Shitski, you nincompoop. Philip adores her.'

'Then why doesn't he say something?'

'He can't.'

'Of course he can! Actors are such cowards. People like Shitski really should be told where to get off.'

'It's not as easy as that. I've spoken to Philip about it, he's very unhappy but he's in a dilemma. He does try to calm Shitski down when he goes into his tantrums, but he thinks it would be counterproductive to make a big scene. He reckons that if he stood up for Natasha, Shitski would take it out on her later in private. He thinks he knocks her around a bit, you see.'

'How perfectly horrid.'

'Oh, he is, he is. Frightful lech as well, takes any opportunity he can to paw at the other actorines. The mystery is why Natasha sticks with him.'

'I was going to ask that myself.'

'Well, I can't answer it. She just seems to block it out. Blind to his faults, knows he's a bastard but forgives him on account of his being a genius.'

'Some women are very odd.'

'Philip says she's a riddle inside an enigma inside a thingum-mywhatsit. He doesn't think she's quite all there. Thinks being with Shitski's unbalanced her.'

'Do you really think he's a genius?'

'Me? Of course I don't. That's what Philip says she says. The woman's clearly a masochist. As Shitski's a sadist some might say they're an ideal couple, but it's a terrible shame; potentially she's such a damned fine actress. I think she's headed for a nervous breakdown. Philip's terrified that's what's going to happen, and that it'll scupper the production.'

'Why's he terrified? If the production's as bad as you say it'd be the best thing all round. Then you can all take an early bath and write it off to experience.'

'Ah, but you don't understand. No matter how bad the rest of it is, Philip is absolutely determined that his own perform-ance will be a knockout. I have to say I haven't seen anything in rehearsals so far to suggest that this will be so, but his single-mindedness is quite wondrous to behold.'

'Why are you whispering? We're not in a library.'

'I am whispering because of the gentleman in the loud shirt who has just arrived not ten seconds ago at the bar. Doesn't he have any other garments in his wardrobe?'

'You mean Dick Jones?'

'Ssh! You can be so indiscreet!'

'You can talk!'

'That has been commented on before ... Anyway, as far as Philip is concerned, the production is irrelevant. What counts is his performance measured against Mr Jones's, and if what you have said is true, then I'd say Jones is already clear of the field by a dozen lengths.'

'He's seen us.'

'I know, he's coming over. Act natural and pretend we were talking about something else ... Ha! Ha! So anyway, Ralph was just coming out of the stage door and was about to climb on to his motorcycle, when who should come up to him but—'

'Good evening, gentlemen. I trust I'm not butting in?'

'Good heavens! Mr Richard Jones himself! *Quel* surprise! Congratulations are in order, I understand.'

'Well, I don't know about that. We'll have to wait for the notices tomorrow.'

'I've no doubt they shall be outstanding. Can I get you a drink?'

'I've had a few already, thanks ... So, Seymour, what did you think?'

'Oh, I'm sorry, I haven't actually seen the show. Only got here twenty minutes ago. Been rehearsing.'

'Ah yes, of course. And how is your little ... enterprise progressing?'

'Mm. Perhaps not quite as smoothly as one might have wished.'

'How delicately phrased! I've heard it's a major balls-up.'

'Oh? And who told you that?'

'A little bird.'

'Strange how many talking varieties there are in London, isn't it? We've had some teething troubles, it's true.'

'Let's hope you overcome them. When did you say you were opening?'

'I didn't. But it's tomorrow.'

'And you've still got – what was the expression you used? Ah yes, "teething troubles". Oh dear . . . Previews go well?'

'We're not having any previews.'

'That is brave!'

'Necessity, I'm afraid, not courage: no time left, what with the rehearsal rescheduling.'

'Ah yes. Dress rehearsal go well then?'

'A few minor hiccups. We're finishing off tomorrow afternoon.'

'Hiccups as well as teething troubles? Sailing a bit close to the wind, aren't we?'

'Best place to sail.'

'All I can say is you'd better watch out for those rocks! Must dash, there's a party. Give my regards to dear, dear Philip . . . Break a leg!'

Seymour pulled a face as Dick Jones left them.

'I thought you handled that pretty well,' said his friend. 'He was being intolerable.'

'Break a leg indeed! I'd like to break his neck . . . Awful thing is, he's got every reason to be smug . . . Finish up, that's the last drink I'll be able to buy here for a while; I shan't dare show my face. We're about to go down with all hands.'

'You mean you're going to hit those rocks he warned you against?'

'My dear, rocks schmocks . . . It's the icebergs I'm worried about.'

# 8

'Howard will see you in a few minutes, Mr Fletcher. Please take a seat.'

Philip mumbled his thanks to Howard Suter's receptionist and considered warily the various skeletal items of modernist furniture on offer. He chose the one that least looked like it had come from the Inquisition's clearance sale. He opened his paper.

'Would you like a coffee while you're waiting?'

Philip shook his head. After five weeks of rehearsal he was awash; his stomach felt like a bilge pump at the end of a voyage. He was a latter-day Prufrock, the shapeless hours had been defined by spoonfuls of Ebony Smooth. He wondered if, like Balzac, he was in danger of succumbing to a caffeine overdose. At least it would be release from the inhuman comedy he was currently enduring.

They were opening tonight.

It was a nightmare. Thinking about it grated his nerves. He started instinctively to reach for his cigarettes, then noticed the sign behind the receptionist's desk. It said: This Office Is A Tobacco-Free Zone. From the blank looks on everyone's faces it looked suspiciously like a Brain-Free Zone as well, but that was another matter. Better for him not to light up anyway, he supposed, dropping the packet back into his pocket. He'd been trying to cut down, he was worried about his voice.

They were opening tonight.

A sharp spasm racked him as he turned the page of his paper. There it was again, the notice he had been trying to avoid lest it induce apoplexy; and possibly the most cringe-making first-night headline in theatrical history:

Philip closed his eyes and breathed deeply, suppressing the urge to vomit. He might be opening tonight, and that was bad enough, but the universally favourable reaction to the talentless scumbag who had opened last night made the impossible intolerable. His hand shook so horribly he could barely decipher the mocking phrases:

'Richard Jones ... staking a claim as perhaps the outstanding classical talent of his generation ... a sharply intelligent reading which makes a notoriously difficult part look easy ... a magnificent speaking voice allied to a powerful natural presence ... privileged to witness these great Shakespearians in their prime ...'

'Bloody bollocks!' Philip muttered furiously. 'Call this a serious newspaper? It's a bloody joke!'

A buzzer sounded on the receptionist's desk.

'Howard will see you now, Philip,' she said, a little uncertainly, perhaps distracted by his not-so-muttered outburst. 'It's through there ...'

Philip slouched off towards the indicated door. He was feeling so cross he wanted to kick it in. He got a grip in time, and used the handle.

'Philip, hi! Be with you right away. Take a seat.'

The young man lying back in his chair with his feet on the desk waved him to a black and chrome arrangement of tubing with a Perspex seat. He lowered himself into it cautiously.

'To hell with the merchandizing percentage, Hank! Tell him he's gotta open his wallet now.'

Howard Suter put his hand over the phone and winked at Philip.

'Sorry about this. Multiple client renegotiation package.'

Philip responded with a minimal nod. A more demonstrative gesture, he felt, might have unbalanced him. He tried to centre himself in the diminutive Perspex seat.

'Hell, Hank, tell him to quit bullshitting. We already compromised on the rolling exercise, six percent's my bottom line. I've got someone here right now, will you get back to me? ... Sure, you have a nice day too.'

Howard Suter waited for the line to go dead before adding: 'Asshole!'

He dropped the phone casually on to the desk and inclined his large sandy head towards Philip. He gave a boyish freckly grin.

'Another day, another million dollars!'

Philip laughed slightly in response. The chrome struts of the Perspex chair trembled.

'So ...' continued the agent, recrossing his legs and folding the gold bracelet on one wrist over the conspicuous Rolex on the other. 'Mr Philip Fletcher. In person. Yup ...'

Howard nodded his head slowly, seriously. Philip presumed he would say something more, but a long silence ensued. He just sat there, still nodding, like a toy animal in the back of a car.

'Well, I didn't think I could send a proxy,' Philip murmured, lamely.

'Nope.'

Howard continued to bore through him with his big, oddly ingenuous blue eyes. Philip felt like a piece of string being stared at by a ginger kitten. Quite suddenly, the agent moved.

'Philip, I'm gonna show you something.'

He pulled his heels off the desk and swivelled his body round to face a computer monitor. He tapped in a keyboard command.

'This is a hi-tech modern agency, Philip. We're state of the art here; only way to keep ahead of the game. This is my client database. As you know, we've got *Spotlight* on CD-ROM now. This is an extension of that technology, but it's much, much more. I'll just call up your page ... here!'

He tapped in some numbers and tilted the screen so that Philip could see. His own photograph, what he called his Ironic Profile, looked back at him.

'As you know, Philip, all your personal details are here. What I'm gonna do now is operate the Casting Conversion Program, or CCP for short. Run the utility, so, and we're ready to shoot. This baby's a penthium, she doesn't hang around. OK now, let's just suppose you're already my client and I want to check out your optimum casting situation. I input your codes from the database ... let's see: Age, that'll be a four seven, that's easy, huh? Nationality, British; we call that an E4, sub-code C for Caucasian. Height? Five one one – some of this is straight digital transference, the rest is from the book. I won't go into detail now, like full driving licence, horseriding skills etc, just the basics. There's an automatic conversion utility, of course, I'm just inputting this manually to show you.'

'Oh, please don't bother yourself on my account –'

'It's no trouble at all, Philip, no trouble at all. I want you to see the way we operate, you got it? Now I'll just save the file, drag-and-click, copy over, easy as a cowgirl on Friday night, and here we are, yup ... we're in CIRCUS. What do you think?'

'CIRCUS? Is that an acronym?'

'Yup. Central Information and Resource Casting Utility Software. This entire agency is CIRCUS-orientated. Pretty impressive, huh?'

'Er, yes. What exactly does it do?'

'Everything. I'll give you a demonstration. This is the Character Breakdown icon. Double-click and up comes the sub-menu, see? Now click on the Cast icon and we get the message "Input File". Now I load you up, click, click, and we're cross-referencing already. Hey, what's this? *Lord of the Manor* – that's the new CBS mini-series they're shooting here in the autumn, big prestige number, let's see what we've got. Right, instruct to printer and zap! Here it comes!'

The printer went clickety-click. Howard ripped off a sheet of perforated green and white paper and thrust it over.

'There! It's your COCO.'

'Come again?'

'Client's Optimum Casting Option. Tell me what it says.'

Philip looked down at the paper. He read aloud: '"Philip should play – Beryl Marples, a 51-year-old cockney domestic."'

'Huh? Give that here!'

The agent snatched back the paper.

'Jeez, I must have input the wrong sex code. Never mind, I can re-type the data and—'

'Howard!' Philip raised a hand dramatically, though the force of the gesture was seriously compromised when he had to lower it at once in order to steady the chair. 'It's all right,' he continued, when he had regained his balance. 'No need, I think I get the picture.'

'Well, if you're sure . . .'

Howard pushed his chair back from the monitor reluctantly. After a moment's thought he leant across the desk and gave Philip a deep meaningful look.

'Let's talk about your career parameters.'

'My what?'

'I want my clients to have a high ambition threshold. I'm looking at a top five-percent QUEASY rating.'

'I'm sorry, you've lost me . . .'

'QUEASY. That's Quotient Utility for the Evaluation and Assessment of Success Yearning. You've gotta want it, Philip. You've gotta want it so bad it hurts.'

'Oh I do, Howard, I do.'

'That's what I like to hear, Philip. This show you're doing at the moment, you're aiming high, right?'

'Well, one does one's best—'

'Only the best is good enough, my friend. *Anthony and Cleopatra* . . . I like the sound of that. That's good, that's high profile, that's sexy. I can relate to it, and do you know why? Because I saw the movie, that's why.'

'The movie? Oh, you mean the Charlton Heston . . . thing.'

'Chuck? Hell, no, he wasn't in it. I'm talking about Liz Taylor. Richard Burton was Anthony, right?'

'Well, it's not exactly the same—'

'Hell no, course it ain't, that was a movie and this is theatre. A lot of agents make the mistake of thinking theatre sucks, but not me, no sirree. Theatre is class, Philip, and class I can sell. In the long run, theatre sucks but class is bucks, you see what I mean? We're talking Prestige Product Placement here, the three p's. Pee, pee, pee! That's my motto!'

'Doesn't quite have the ring of *Honi soit qui mal y pense*, say ...'

'Sorry, Philip, I didn't do Latin. Now listen up there. I'm gonna tell you how the agency operates ...'

Do you have to? thought Philip. But obviously he did.

It took Philip another twenty minutes before he could extricate himself from the interview. He stopped off in Soho at one of his regular haunts, but there was no one in the bar he knew. He went to a newsagent's and flipped through the review sections. They were all full of ludicrous panegyrics and sickly waffling hyperbole. Why, oh why, had he not murdered Jones when he'd had the chance? Reluctantly he hailed a cab and headed off for Hammersmith. He began to take out his cigarettes, then noticed the 'Thank You For Not Smoking' sign. He declined to give a tip.

He wasn't called till two o'clock, but Shitski had been rehearsing other scenes since midday. It was lunchtime, but he felt too nervous for food. Instead he bought himself a small medicinal Scotch. Melissa Pine was sitting at the table nearest the bar, scribbling keenly in a notebook.

'Another job application?' Philip asked pleasantly.

'I'm very happy with the one I've got, thank you,' she answered primly.

Philip sighed. If she hadn't been so unremittingly serious she would have been distinctly fanciable. It was painful to see such promising raw material wasted.

'Have you seen Sergei?' she asked, putting down her pen.

'No,' he answered distractedly. His sex life was non-existent at the moment. He had tried to chat up Sally, but that had been a complete waste of time. Was he losing his touch? Worse, was he past it? It was a worrying thought, to add to all the other worrying thoughts he'd been having lately. Sex was his hobby. It was the only thing apart from fame and money which really interested him.

'Sergei's promised me another interview,' said Melissa

eagerly. 'I want to talk to him about the end of the play. I think his interpretation's fascinating.'

Philip hoped that if she were successful in prising any insights out of the director then she would be good enough to pass them on to the cast. None of them had a clue what was meant to be going on at the end of the production. It would be typical of Sergei to tell her and not them. He and Melissa were always going off together, she with her wretched tape recorder in hand, to conduct yet another fatuous in-depth interview. Life, as far as she was concerned, seemed to amount to little more than a series of out-takes from *The Late Show*.

'He has such clarity of vision,' Melissa insisted, her voice breathy with reverence. 'Such artistic coherence.'

Philip decided that if he had to listen to any more of this drivel he was going to be ill. Melissa's eyes were glowing, mere mention of Sergei had been enough to animate her. Philip knocked back his Scotch, bid her a hasty adieu and stomped off grumpily towards the auditorium.

What on earth was the attraction of Sergei Shustikov? Not just to Melissa (she was young, not long out of university, her head stuffed with academic nonsense), but to Natasha. He treated Natasha abominably, why did she put up with it? Why had she chosen him in the first place? She could have had anyone. She could have had him.

He lit a cigarette. He felt on edge, depressed. An opening night was a time of compressed torture, a nerve-racking ordeal which always made him vulnerable. His various insecurities queued up to plague him. Why had he suddenly become so unattractive to the opposite sex? He was surrounded by desirable women, why did none of them fancy him? He felt like a starving pauper in a French pastry shop.

The stage was empty. A few of the actors were sitting around, awaiting their calls. Philip went to join Seymour, who was alone at the back.

'How's it going?' he asked disconsolately.

'Guess . . . How was your interview?'

'Awful. I don't know where they get them from. Looks like I'm stuck with John Quennell.'

'Better the devil you know.'

'Where's Shitski?'

'Went off in a tantrum a couple of minutes ago. Lighting director ballsed up a cue. Not his fault, but at least you could see what Shitski was complaining about. Most of the time he just blows up for no reason.'

'Like Richie Calvi, eh?'

'And look what happened to him . . .'

Philip grunted. Some eighteen months had passed since he had found the unpleasant Mr Calvi stabbed to death in his dressing room on opening night in Bath. Philip could think of no one, with the possible exception of Jones the unmentionable, who deserved the same fate as richly as Shitski. Would nobody rid them of this turbulent tsar?

At last Shitski reappeared, wearing a scowl like a deep-sea trench. The cast reassembled in the wings at the stage manager's call.

'Did you say you wanted to do Act IV, scene viii first?' asked the stage manager respectfully.

'Later,' growled Shitski. 'Banquet now. Where the hell are actors?'

The director did not believe in rehearsal schedules. He was forever changing his mind about the order of work, he seemed to relish catching them out. The delay while the full cast was assembled fuelled his filthy mood.

'Nice to see you!' he jeered sarcastically at the sheepish latecomers. 'You think you work for damn British Rail, or what?'

The cast huddled together for mutual support. There were a lot of them, the combined trains of Antony, Octavius and Pompey, fleshed out with every spare actor. The scene was set on Pompey's ship.

Unfortunately there wasn't much on the set to suggest a nautical flavour. The sandpit downstage was zealously reserved for the Egyptians, which left the polystyrene wastes at the back for everyone else. Centre stage was largely taken up by the rusty Ford Cortina, and the rest of the playing area was awkwardly cordoned off by oddly angled pieces of scaffolding and random piles of household waste: literally, since Shitski had personally directed the crew while they ransacked the theatre bins and festooned the stage with their spoils. Philip's abiding fear was that the abundance of rubbish might serve as an uncomfortably accurate motif for the production as a whole.

Shitski's answer to the nautical question had been radical: he had instructed the costume mistress to furnish the actor playing Pompey with a sailor's cap. The torn strip of bloody sheet hanging from a metal spar at the back might have hinted at a sail. The company crowded beneath it, perched on assorted cardboard boxes and aluminium beer kegs. What any of it had to do with either Shakespeare or the particular play in question was a mystery known only to the director.

'Lepidus exit shit,' he declared to them gnomically, when they had all taken their positions.

Poor Charlie, the ancient character actor playing the part, looked terrified. Halfway through the scene he was meant to be carried over to the other side of the stage in a drunken stupor and hung up from a meat hook by means of a special harness worn under his dinner jacket. He was taken down and dragged off by the heels at the end of the scene, but Sergei had mused aloud during the technical rehearsal that it might perhaps be better to leave him suspended there until the interval. Charlie was taking the threat very seriously indeed.

'Hang like carcass, dead animal, is wrong,' the director snarled at him, as if implying that the idea had been Charlie's in the first place. 'Have new idea. New image. Do lines. Now!'

They all knew Sergei well enough by now not to risk stoking his anger by dithering. The two young actors detailed to carry Charlie picked him up smartly, and Seymour launched into the scene: 'There's a strong fellow, Menas.'

'Why?' Menas answered.

Charlie was carried out of the semi-circle of beer kegs.

'Go to car!' Shitski commanded. Then, to Seymour: 'Get on with it!'

Seymour obliged:

*Enobarbus.* 'A bears the third part of the world, man, see'st
      not?
*Menas.* The third part, then, is drunk; would it were all,
      That it might go on wheels!

'Stop!' the director bellowed at Lepidus's porters. 'Put him
in car!'

The two young men exchanged looks.

'In the front or the back?' asked the bolder of the
two.

'In back, of course! He is backseat driver. Antony and Caesar
fight for steering wheel.'

'Not literally, I hope,' commented Philip uneasily.

'Nah! Is metaphor, for Christ sake. My little joke, you
understand? Menas say he go on wheels. Car go on wheels. I
put him in car. Good joke, no?'

No, Philip thought to himself, while nodding his polite
agreement. If the jokes were usually that bad in Russia, no
wonder the country was in such a mess.

'Now get off!' Shitski ordered brusquely. 'Where is
Natasha? Now I do scene eight.'

Everyone bar Philip and the three actors who made up his
glorious conquering army in Act IV left the stage.

'Natasha make shit late entrance,' grumbled Shitski. 'Scene
lousy upstage.'

Philip nodded. He had had to play half the scene in the
dress rehearsal with his back to the audience. For all his faults,
Shitski's basic stagecraft was sound.

'I'm sorry, Philip,' said Natasha, appearing in the wings. 'I
didn't hear the cue yesterday.'

'Bah!' Shitski scoffed from his seat in the front row of the
audience. 'Clean shit ears, damn you!'

'I'll give it to you strongly,' said Philip quickly, trying not
to give her time to register her lover's unpleasantness. He
smiled at her encouragingly. She looked as if she needed all
the encouragement she could get. 'I'll go back a couple of
lines, all right?'

Philip took up a centre-stage position on the sand, in front

of the absurd Ford Cortina. He waited for the others to settle
before beginning.

> ...Tell them your feats; whilst they with joyful tears
> Wash the congealment from your wounds, and kiss
> The honour'd gashes whole...

He saw Natasha coming on out of the corner of his eye.
He gestured to Martin, the actor playing Scarus:

> ...Give me thy hand;
> To this great fairy I'll commend thy acts...

Unfortunately, just as he turned, Philip caught a glimpse of
Seymour in the wings waving a limp wrist and doing his
famous spot-on impression of a great fairy. Martin snickered
and Philip's own voice cracked. He recovered and shot a
withering glance at the irrepressible Loseby, who affected
not to notice. Philip hated this bloody speech and he was not
looking forward to the schools matinees: the great fairy
was bad enough, but to a puerile audience (and Seymour)
the end of the speech was even worse. Philip steeled his
concentration as Natasha came gliding across the stage towards him:

> ...leap thou, attire and all,
> Through proofs of harness to my heart, and there
> Ride on the pants triumphing.

Martin and the others began spluttering uncomfortably
through their noses: in the wings, Seymour had dropped his
trousers and was pulling quizzically at the elastic of his jockey
shorts. Seeing their strained faces, Natasha stopped and
glanced back over her shoulder.

'What shit you do!' screamed the demented Russian out
front. 'What kind shit crap actress are you?'

Natasha stepped back nervously as Shitski bounded on

to the stage. He bore down on her like a battleship at full steam.

'You shit useless amateur crap actress or what?' he yelled.

'I'm so-sorry—' she stammered.

Philip attempted to interject: 'It's not Natasha's fault, Sergei, I'm afraid it's mine, I—'

But Shitski wasn't listening.

'You shit useless English bitch!' he screamed, thrusting his shaggy red face into hers and waving his fist under her nose. She turned her cheek and wiped the corner of her eye.

'Sergei, you're . . . dribbling.'

'Bah!'

He took a very deliberate step backwards, and stared at her with contempt. Then he spat into her face.

There was a collective gasp from all onlookers. Like the others, Philip was momentarily stunned. He had never seen such appalling nastiness. Suddenly, all the martinets, sadists and psychopaths he had encountered during his career masquerading as members of the Directors' Guild seemed like so many spring lambs. This monster of the steppes was the genuine article.

'You bastard,' said Natasha, and slapped his face.

It was a moot point which was the more surprised, Natasha or Shitski. Probably Shitski, Philip reflected. For anyone to stand against him was unprecedented; for her to do so was tantamount to revolution.

'Bitch!' Shitski gasped. He raised his fist.

Natasha kicked him in the balls. His bright-red cheeks went purple and his face contorted like an oxygen-starved diver's. He collapsed in an inert emasculated heap on to the floor. And someone started clapping.

Whoever began it was safely anonymous in the darkened wings, but it spread into the open like contagious measles: the smattering of cast members in the stalls took it up; Martin and the pitiful Antonine army swelled the noise; and Philip smote his palms as gustily as anyone. The applause fed Natasha, she seemed to grow where she stood. She looked down at the pained heap of a man before her with disdain.

'Up yours!' she said with that long-buried but still potent stylishness that Philip remembered so well. She stood quivering with her unleashed emotions for a moment more, then turned and exited gloriously like Bernhardt in her prime.

The clapping intensified; cheers and catcalls sang out. Shitski remained immobile on the floor, rooted by shock and pain. He opened his mouth and tried to say something, but no sound came out. He looked crushed.

'We've got a performance in a few hours,' Philip said to the stage manager. 'I don't think anyone's in the mood to rehearse.'

The stage manager nodded crisply. It was clear that someone needed to take control; Shitski's loss of moral authority had been instant and absolute.

'The half's at six twenty-five, everyone,' said the stage manager. 'Good luck!'

Matter-of-factly he offered Shitski a hand. The director looked at him blankly, like a road accident victim too bewildered to take anything in. His whole world had just been turned upside-down. He looked around vaguely, as if seeking support, but everyone was turning away.

'Philip!' he gasped.

But Philip ignored him. He was already walking offstage, after Natasha.

'What's going on?' demanded Melissa Pine, leaping out of the wings and fumbling with her microphone. Philip smiled grimly. After all those hours of worthless recording, was it possible that she had missed the only genuinely dramatic moment in rehearsals?

'Just a little local difficulty,' he answered smoothly. 'Excuse me, please . . .'

He hurried on out of the auditorium after Natasha. The company was too big for everyone to fit into the main-house dressing rooms, so half of them had been put in the Studio Theatre, Natasha included. Her door was open, and the costume mistress was sitting on the sofa sewing a button.

'She's gone already,' she informed him. 'Said she was going out.'

There was a side exit from the Studio that led into River Terrace. Philip reached it just in time to see Natasha turning the corner into Crisp Road. He caught up with her, took her by the arm, and frogmarched her over the road.

'Where are you taking me?' she asked.

He nodded towards the pub. 'I don't know about you, but I need a stiff drink...'

# 9

The pub was empty; the barman had to be summoned from within. Philip ordered drinks and carried them over to the corner Natasha had chosen. He handed her an unadulterated brandy.

'I'm sorry, Philip, I just couldn't take any more. I snapped.'

She knocked back her drink aggressively; it set her coughing.

'Would you like another?' he asked, giving her his handkerchief. She shook her head.

'Better not, thanks. We're performing in a few hours ... Oh God. Oh God! Philip, what's going to become of us?'

She threw her face into the handkerchief and began crying. They were not gentle tears, but violent sobs. She had been wound up so tight that now it came flooding out. He put an arm round her and she responded by sinking her head into his chest. He didn't say anything, he just waited for her to empty herself.

'I'm sorry,' she said at last, lifting her face and, reluctantly, lowering the damp handkerchief. 'I must look a mess.'

'No.'

He meant it truthfully, not just for reassurance's sake. Yes, she was red-eyed and her mascara had run, but she seemed to have sloughed off some of her debilitating nervy paleness. She seemed human again.

'I'm surprised you stuck it as long as you did,' he said. 'It's been very hard standing on the sidelines, watching the way he treated you. I wanted to intervene, I'm sorry I didn't, I felt like a coward—'

'No, you would have made it worse.'

'I thought that too, but it was still cowardly of me.'

'No, Philip, it was something I had to do for myself. You don't understand, do you?'

'Don't I? Well, I think I do, actually. So did everyone else, that's why we applauded.'

'No, I don't mean my hitting him. Poor Sergei, I'm afraid I kicked him rather hard. I mean, you don't understand why I didn't do it earlier. Why I've put up with him so long. Why I'm with him in the first place.'

'I must confess, Natasha, I had come to the conclusion that your true métier might be something in the kamikaze line.'

Her laugh was rueful but unforced, a contrast to the tight-lipped smiles which had been her trademark of late. She squeezed his hand affectionately.

'I've been in a state, I'm afraid. When I met Sergei I was at a low ebb. I think I was on the verge of a nervous breakdown. He took pity on me. I was grateful.'

Philip could barely withhold a wince as he imagined the scene. Shitski must have smelt her vulnerability like a sweet perfume; a vulture nosing fresh meat.

'. . . I was so low when I met him I was actually thinking of killing myself. It's terrible, I know, Philip, but everything had gone wrong. I'd split up with Jack after five years – you didn't know Jack, did you?'

Philip shook his head.

'. . . And then I discovered I was pregnant. It was awful, I'd been longing for a child all those years with Jack, it was one of the things that drove us apart. I couldn't believe the irony of it. I wanted us to get back together again, but it was too late, he'd found someone else, I fell into the most awful depression, and then . . . Oh God, I lost the baby. You don't have another handkerchief, do you?'

As it happened he had some tissues, but they were scarcely adequate: a whole Kleenex factory would have been needed to mop her up.

'There, there,' he said, squeezing her hand back awkwardly. He knew it was a pretty pathetic thing to say, but it was still the best he could manage: the emotional life was not his forte.

'Oh God, I'm sorry, Philip. You don't want to listen to all this, it's not fair.'

'No, that's fine,' he lied uncomfortably. 'Get it off your chest!'

He was thinking about the play. Would she have anything left to give tonight? Her performance was so anaemic already it was difficult to imagine it becoming any more feeble, but, nonetheless, he doubted that this was the best preparation. It certainly wasn't what he wanted for himself.

'It'll be fabulous tonight!' he said decisively. 'I'm sure it's all going to gel.'

But she didn't want to change the subject.

'Philip, you've no idea how awful it is. I'm desperate for a child, absolutely desperate. I'm thirty-eight years old. That means I'm going to be forty in two years' time, and then it'll be too late.'

'Really?' he said faintly. If there was one subject in the world on which he was unqualified to offer advice, this was probably it. 'Can't medical science do wonderful things these days?'

'Oh, it's bad enough in your thirties, Philip. It's the battle career women are having to face every day of their lives. I know there are exceptions, but once you're turned forty you're as good as past it.'

'Yes?'

As someone who was closer to fifty than to forty, he felt reluctant to endorse this as a general proposition.

'You don't know what it's like being a woman.'

As Philip didn't, he could not in fairness demur. He remained silent.

'That's why I wanted to kill myself!' she said suddenly, fiercely. 'It was the last straw, I was really going to do it, you know . . .'

Philip's blank look became an expressionless black hole. For him it was a toss-up which was the more alarming subject, pregnancy or suicide. A manic glint had come into her eyes.

'Here,' she said mysteriously, tapping a silver locket she wore round her neck. She opened it with her fingernails and drew out of the cavity a cellophane-wrapped white capsule, which she held up to the light. The word POISON was conspicuously stamped across it.

'Cyanide,' she said, quietly for maximum dramatic impact.

'At least wait until you've read the notices,' he tried gamely. She gave her head a solemn shake.

'It's all right, I'm not going to take it now. I've had it for years, it was my insurance policy. I just wanted you to know I meant it . . .'

He attempted another light smile. It wasn't easy, his natural urbanity was being stretched to the limit. He felt a cold clamminess in his spine, a symphony of trembling in his limbs: he had known she was on the edge, but how had he not noticed that he'd been working with a full-blown suicidal depressive these past five weeks? One more shove and Shitski could have tipped her over – and then what?

'Nothing. Finito. The end.'

'What did you say, Philip?'

'Oh, nothing. I'm sorry, my mind was wandering . . .'

Wandering to thoughts of the unspeakable Jones and his ghastly, over-praised performance. What were his chances of outshining him now? What had they ever been? Minimal, he supposed, taking a sip of his drink as if out of a poisoned chalice. He was relieved to see that she had returned the cyanide pill to the locket.

'I know what you must think of Sergei, Philip. But I want him to father my child.'

'Ah . . .' Philip stared with renewed gloom at his near-empty glass. Perhaps it would taste better with the cyanide in after all. 'It's not really my place to say, I know, but he doesn't exactly strike me as the paternal sort.'

'He's not, but he's agreed to it. I know what you must think of him, but . . . I haven't got time to waste, Philip, my biological clock is running out. He's promised, after this production. He'll give me a baby then.'

Philip hoped that her kick to his groin had not seriously affected his prospects.

'I realize he's erratic, temperamental – all right, he's a complete bastard, I know that, Philip, you don't need to tell me, but . . . but you have to understand the kind of life he led in the past. He had a terrible time in Russia, you know.'

Didn't everyone? Philip had always assumed. Surely that was the point of Russia . . .

'. . . He was like a caged animal in Moscow. He's an artist, he needs space, creative freedom. He's been given that in the west, but he's a perfectionist, he doesn't tolerate fools gladly, and people just can't understand that. Won't understand him. He's a good man, you know, deep down.'

Very, very deep down, Philip decided.

'I really do think he's brilliant. A second Stanislavsky. We just haven't seen the best of him in this production. Do you know he's been invited to Bristol on Friday to open the new Stanislavsky Centre there? He's unveiling a plaque, it's very fitting. I hope I'll be able to go with him. It's at midday, the trains are good, I don't see why I can't get back in time for the evening show, I . . .'

She was rambling. He stopped listening. She had that post-Messianic look in her eyes again; or, as he saw it, the despair of a reluctant rationalist clinging out of fear and habit to a moribund faith. He could only pray that her spark of rebellion hadn't been a flash in the pan. He had interpreted her act of defiance as the snapping of an evil enchantment, as in the grimmest of fairy tales, but it seemed that it would take more than one bound for her to be free. At least he knew now that she had it in her. And he understood her a little better. He could see how the investment she had made in Sergei Shustikov was so great that the truth of its worthlessness was too much for her to accept. He could see how she had painted herself into an emotional corner, and how each further stroke of the brush merely made her shut her eyes the tighter. He had had some slight experience of female broodiness before, but hers was a very severe case, and it made her vulnerability to the monstrous linchpin of her life acute.

Eventually she stopped talking. She sat staring emptily at the wall, an occasional tremor crossing her face. Each passing moment made him dread the coming ordeal still more.

'What's the time?' she asked faintly, after an uncomfortable silence.

'It's nearly six.'

'Do you know what sales are like?'

'Advance is fair. Tonight's full.'

'A lot of paper, I expect.'

She meant that the audience would be fleshed out with complimentary-ticket holders, a genus which always laughed too loudly and clapped too enthusiastically. He doubted if even their best efforts would fool the critics tonight.

'I think I'd like to get back,' he said.

'I'll come with you. I'd prefer not to be alone.'

'I'll be there . . .'

It was obvious she was worried about Shitski, and who could blame her? Philip doubted that the Russian's reaction next time he saw her was going to be pleasant. The physical blow she had given him could be repaid, but not the figurative one: she had humiliated him, and Philip was quite sure that he had never experienced anything like it. She needed minding tonight and, much as he would have preferred to have time to prepare on his own, he knew that he did not dare leave her alone with him. Her grip on sanity might not withstand another all-out assault.

They went back over the road. Natasha held his hand.

'Would you mind coming to my dressing room for a while?'

He nodded. It was more comfortable than his.

'I'll join you in a second,' he said. 'I just want to collect some things.'

Actors like to prepare for performances in different ways. Some need to go endlessly over the lines, a process of Stanislavskian exhaustion. Philip preferred to try to empty his mind and relax, relying on the hard work done in rehearsal to waken his instincts when the curtain rose. In that grey time between arriving at the theatre and putting on his make-up and costume, he liked to read or listen to music, anything to create an illusion of tranquillity. He went, therefore, to his dressing room to pick up his Walkman and was just choosing some tapes when Seymour rushed in dramatically.

'Philip! We were looking for you everywhere! We've just had an Equity meeting. We decided we're not going to put up with Shitski's bullying for a moment longer and we passed a motion of solidarity!'

Seymour was such bad casting for the role of union agitator that Philip was a little taken aback.

'I think we should try to avoid any confrontation just at the moment,' he said tentatively, when he had come to terms with Seymour's outbreak of Scargillism. 'For Natasha's sake, if not ours. She's so on edge, we really mustn't put any more pressure on her.'

'Turning the other cheek hasn't done us much good so far, has it, Philip?'

'True, but . . .' Philip hesitated. He knew the others resented the preferential treatment he had been getting. 'Perhaps I should have a word,' he said reluctantly. 'Do you know where Shitski is?'

'Last time I saw him he was in Natasha's dressing room.'

'What?'

'I said—'

'Out of the way!'

Philip threw down his Walkman and rushed out, almost bowling his old friend over. He tore down the corridor, through the pass door and across the foyer to the Studio Theatre. As he raced through the door to the dressing rooms he heard a terrible stabbing scream.

'You shit never knock?' Shitski yelled, his thick bass growl all but drowned out by Natasha's hysterical sobs. Philip dispensed with the formality of knocking himself.

'Oh my God . . .'

He stood panting in the doorway, hearing the frantic beating of his heart even above the ghastly racket. One look was enough to see what it was all about, and it was much worse than he could have imagined.

Shitski was lying on the comfortable dressing-room couch, wearing as smug and insolent an expression as a man can possibly get away with when he is in the undignified position of having his trousers round his ankles. Melissa Pine, in a matching state of undress, was climbing out from under him.

'You bastard!' gasped Natasha, and then, to Melissa: 'Bitch . . .'

Melissa Pine set about covering her limbs. She took her cue from Shitski, and tried to assume a casual unperturbed air.

'You might at least close the door,' she said frostily, fishing in her bag for a cigarette. 'This isn't a public show, you know.'

But it was. Half the cast was gathering outside, perhaps suffering from restricted view but with little left to the imagination. Seymour came waddling eagerly round the corner to join them.

'How dare you!' hissed Natasha, though whether the rebuke was aimed at Shitski or Melissa was hard to tell. She seemed faint to the point of collapse. Philip put a steadying arm round her. He glanced quickly behind him.

'All right, everyone,' he said, winking at Seymour. 'Let's all get ready for the show . . .'

Seymour understood, reluctantly. He set about dispersing the crowd. Philip gave Natasha another supportive squeeze.

'Come and use my dressing room,' he said urgently. 'I'll ask them to bring your costume through —'

'No!'

Natasha broke free. She took a furious step towards the two miscreants on the couch, who were in the final stages of rebuttoning.

'How dare you! How bloody dare you, you awful nasty sadistic man!'

'Put shit sock in it, woman!' replied her aptly named paramour, with an unmistakable gloat in his voice.

'You did this deliberately, didn't you, to humiliate me? I can't believe even you would go this far, in my dressing room, with this star-fucking little trollop —'

'Don't talk to me like that!' squealed Melissa indignantly, jumping off the couch. She waved a fist at Natasha and Philip caught hold of it.

'Come on you!' he said decisively. 'Out!'

He had her off-balance, and she was powerless to resist as he pulled open the door and shoved her out in one fluent movement.

'Take your hands off me!' Melissa yelped.

There were still a few people out in the corridor, obviously eavesdropping but pretending not to. Philip pressed her into the corner.

'Just shut up and get out!' he demanded through gritted teeth. 'You've done enough damage.'

'What the hell's it got to do with you?' she demanded back, by now red-faced and tearful, all pretence at coolness gone.

'Have you got no brains at all, you ridiculous young woman! Natasha's practically on the edge of a nervous breakdown and there you are shagging her boyfriend in her dressing room, practically making a public show of it an hour before our first performance!'

'It's hardly my fault if she doesn't give him what he needs—'

'What he needs is a bullet through the head.'

'Don't talk about him like that, he's a genius!'

'What is it with you women? He's not a genius, he's a complete arsehole, and he's almost driven poor Natasha to suicide. Do you know she carries a cyanide pill around with her the whole time? That's how close to the edge she is!'

'Huh!' Melissa scoffed. 'What a nutter. Remind me not to let her mix me any drinks.'

'Might not be a bad idea at that,' he said coldly.

'Get shit off me, stupid woman!' Shitski roared dementedly.

Philip turned away from Melissa. The dressing-room door had fallen shut, and through it came incoherent wails from Natasha and ominous thumping sounds. Philip grabbed for the door handle, but it wouldn't budge.

'Oh my God, it's locked! He'll kill her!'

The door shook as something smashed against it.

'Might not be a bad idea!' sniffed Melissa, self-consciously turning on her heels and flouncing down the corridor, aware of every eye behind every open dressing-room door upon her. Philip was the only one paying her no attention.

'Open up!' he demanded uselessly, battering the door with

his fists. But they were making so much noise inside they couldn't have heard him anyway.

'Front of House manager's got a passkey,' said Seymour, appearing by his shoulder at the optimum dramatic moment.

Philip rushed out to the manager's office. No one was in, but the desk was filled with keys of all description. It took him a good minute to locate the right one. When he got back, Seymour was standing with his ear pressed to the door.

'It's all gone deathly quiet!' he told Philip in an eager whisper.

Philip took his arm and pulled him gently away.

'I really think we shouldn't hassle them,' he said firmly. 'Natasha's paranoid enough already, let's give her some space, all right?'

Reluctantly Seymour retreated. Philip knocked on the door. 'Natasha?'

There was no answer, but he heard a muffled sob. He turned the key in the lock and went in.

'Natasha, are you OK . . .'

His voice caught in his throat. Natasha was sitting on the floor in the corner, her knees up to her chin and her hands pressed into her head. There was a nasty cut above one eye, but apart from that she did look OK. She was not the problem, Philip decided, as he carefully reclosed the door after him and equally carefully relocked it. The problem was Shitski.

Shitski's problem was that he was dead.

# *10*

For someone of his age and background, Philip had seen a disproportionately high number of dead bodies. Enough, at least, to know one when he saw it.

Shitski was lying on his side on the couch, facing Philip. His knees were doubled up into his stomach and both hands were limply round his own throat. His eyes were two huge immobile globes. He was well stiffed.

Philip leant back against the door, took deep breaths and tried to clear his head. Carefully he dropped the passkey into his pocket.

'Oh God!' Natasha murmured into her knees. 'What have I done?'

A good question, thought Philip. There was no blood, no sign of force that he could see. Shitski was a powerful brute of a man. How had she killed him?

He had to take deep breaths again. The consequences of that question catalysed his pulse. He was sharing a room with a murderer. And he should know.

He walked carefully into the centre of the room. There was a broken glass and a liquid stain on the floor by one leg of the couch. His toe nudged a shard.

'I poisoned him,' said Natasha quietly.

It was the absolute dead calm in her voice which shocked him most. The tears had dried up, she must have exhausted her emotions. She just sat there in the corner, perfectly still, her chin on her knees and no expression at all on her face.

'You did what?' Philip said, after a stunned pause.

'Poisoned him. We were fighting. I pushed his head back against the wall, then he threw me down here and kicked me.

Screamed his head off, then said I'd given him a shit headache, that was my fault too. I said, here, I've got an aspirin . . .'

She was holding the locket round her neck between one finger and thumb. It was open, and it was empty. Philip looked down incredulously at the body on the couch. Did Russian headache pills usually come with POISON stamped on them in bas-relief? Could the victim's stupidity be any kind of defence? He imagined the scene:

'M'lud . . .' he began in his head, patting down his white horsehair wig with one hand (courtroom props were an actor's gift) and taking hold of the lapel of his gown with the other. 'M'lud, my client handed the cyanide to the deceased accidentally, only realizing afterwards that her boxes of aspirin and poison pills had somehow become intermingled in her handbag . . .'

'In her handbag?' he interrupted himself, doing the judge as Edith Evans. He couldn't think of a suitable reply. The judge had a point.

No, that wouldn't wash at all. How about:

'M'lud, Mr Shustikov's sudden suicide came as a complete surprise to my client, who just happened to be in the room at the time—'

'Philip, what are you talking about?'

He had not been aware of speaking aloud. Nonetheless, he didn't like being interrupted.

'I'm trying to think,' he snapped. 'Trying to think of a way out of this mess.'

There was a sudden loud knocking on the door behind him. It did nothing to lower his heart-rate.

'Is everything all right in there?' demanded Seymour from the other side.

Philip rapidly clocked the positions of Natasha and the corpse and worked out the sight lines. He pulled the key out of his pocket, strode over to the door and unlocked it. He shoved his nose out through a three-inch crack.

'For God's sake, Seymour, piss off and leave us alone!' he hissed. 'They're just having a quiet heart to heart and sorting things out.'

'I'm terribly sorry—' Seymour blurted. Philip slammed the door in his face and locked it again.

'And no eavesdropping!' he shouted sternly through the door.

'What are you doing, Philip?' Natasha demanded colourlessly, from her corner. 'Why don't you call the police, get it over with?'

'Shut up!' said Philip crossly. He began to pace up and down the room, muttering to himself. 'Blast! Why did I tell Melissa about the cyanide? There's no mileage in self-defence. Giving poison, that's premeditated. It's also calculated, we'll never show diminished responsibility. Bugger it!'

He stopped in front of Natasha. At least some expression – it was alarm – had come back into her eyes.

'If you were going to murder him couldn't you at least have waited?' he demanded angrily.

'Waited?' she repeated faintly.

'Yes. Waited till after the first night. It's very selfish of you.'

He recommenced his pacing. The room was small, and every time he finished a circuit he brushed against Shitski's feet.

'Bloody hell! What am I meant to do now?'

He sat down heavily on the dressing-room table and folded his arms. He stared morosely at Shitski's corpse.

'I'm sorry, Philip, I don't understand . . .' Natasha sounded bewildered; it was her little-girl-lost voice. 'I didn't mean to kill him, I'm sorry I did, really I am, but I was so angry, and so humiliated, and I know he did it on purpose, he wanted me to find him in here with her, he wanted everyone to know, he always wanted everyone to know with what contempt he treated me, he . . . Oh God, I'm sorry, I don't know what came over me, I just couldn't take any more. I'm such a fool, I've been deluding myself, I know, it's all my own fault, I should never have let it get as far as it did. Please, Philip, have you got another handkerchief? Philip? What are you doing?'

He was pushing the couch back against the wall. It was heavy, it wouldn't budge easily. When he had got it in as tightly as he could manage, he bent over the corpse's head and closed the bulbous eyes.

'No one's to come into this dressing room, no one at all,' Philip commanded crisply. A folded camel-coloured rug lay across the back of the couch. He shook it out and covered the top half of the body. 'If anybody asks, Shitski's sleeping. Got that?'

'What?'

'Don't give me that cow-like vacant look, Natasha, this is an emergency. For Christ's sake, pull yourself together, we've got a performance in under an hour.'

'A perfor . . . are you jok —'

'Of course I'm bloody not joking! Do I look like I'm bloody joking?'

She recoiled from his sudden outburst of temper. He got a grip on himself and lowered his voice.

'Natasha, what do you want me to do? Call the police? If I call the police, you go to prison. It's as simple as that. We're not talking about months here, you know, or even a few years – we're talking a very long time. Life imprisonment. Think about it.'

'But I didn't mean —'

'Oh, that's going to sound awfully good in court, isn't it? "I'm sorry, my lord, I didn't mean to." How can you accident-ally give someone a cyanide pill? Think about it! There isn't going to be the slightest doubt how he got it, you know. You will be thrown into the darkest dungeon in England, like Mr Toad.' ·

Natasha's lip quivered.

'I'll never be able to have children then . . .'

'Natasha, you seriously need to re-examine your priorities. You have just murdered your lover. This is no time to be thinking of motherhood.'

She burst into tears again. She went to bury her face in her hands but Philip seized her by the wrists and dragged them away none too gently. He slapped her cheek.

'What did you do that for?' she demanded, a flash of spirit in her at last.

'No more time for self-pity, dear,' he said caustically. 'A little lecture, Natasha. Rule of life number one: if you're not prepared to live with the consequences of your actions, don't commit the actions. Now what's it going to be? Shall I call the cops, or are you going to help me? Think carefully. I doubt if sharing a cell for twenty years with a succession of butch felonious types is quite your cup of tea, and, as you say, it'll mean no shopping trips to Mothercare for you – stop it! Start crying again and I'll really belt you. Get a grip, we have a first-night public turning up shortly.'

'But, Philip! You can't expect me to act!'

'Oh, can't I? If you won't, who will? For all I know, Sally's a perfectly good understudy, but she's at least ten years too young for the part and I'm not buying it. The critics will be there tonight and I need you. I'm not giving in to Dick Jones without a fight.'

'So that's it!'

She jumped up from the floor, eyes flashing and cheeks hot with anger.

'That's what it's all about, is it, Philip? You couldn't give a damn about me, could you? Much less poor Sergei, lying there and growing colder by the minute –'

'Ssh! Keep your voice down!'

'I will not! All you care about is some petty professional rivalry. You were always jealous of Dick –'

'Oh no I wasn't –'

'Oh yes you were, and you're not in the bloody pantomime now! You're just using me, like . . . like he did!'

She indicated the body on the couch with a gesture of scornful dismissal. Philip was stung.

'How can you compare me with him? I'm trying to help, get you out of this ridiculous hole you've dug for yourself. God, you've got awful taste in men!'

'You mean because I wouldn't go to bed with you?'

'Your loss, dear.'

'That's not what I've heard.'

'Bitch! No wonder he knocked you about.'

'I'm sorry. I just said that.'

94

'I know.'

'Why did you call me a bitch then?'

'I'm sorry, I just said it.'

'I know . . . Philip, I'm sorry I treated you so badly.'

'Did you? When?'

'Of course I did. In Bristol. I treated you terribly.'

'It wasn't your fault.'

'Oh, I was very young, I know, but I played up to it. I played with you too. I knew how much you fancied me.'

'Still do.'

'You don't mean that.'

'Yes I do, and don't say, "No you don't!" This isn't the bloody pantomime.'

'Philip?'

'Yes?'

'I'm sorry.'

'You've said that already.'

'I mean for getting you into this mess. I'm sorry I killed Sergei.'

'I don't think I'm the one you should be apologizing to.'

'There's not a lot to be gained from apologizing to him, is there?'

'I take your point.'

'Philip?'

'Yes?'

'What are we going to do?'

'I'm thinking about it.'

'I don't want to go to prison.'

'I guessed as much.'

'Philip?'

'Still me.'

'The other day in rehearsals . . . did you really mean it when you said you wanted to screw me?'

'Yes.'

'You weren't just saying it to make me feel better?'

'I just admitted I still fancy you. What more do you want?'

'Philip?'

'Yes?'

'I'd like you to know: I fancy you too.'

'You do?'

'I do.'

'Oh.'

'Is that all you can say?'

'It's a little unexpected.'

'What are we going to do next?'

'I'm not sure.'

'Will you kiss me while you think about it?'

'If you insist.'

They grabbed for each other like a pair of turbo-charged vacuum cleaners. Their lips bruised, their tongues clashed, their hands clawed and tore. Fifteen years of concentrated suppressed lust consumed Philip; his vision grew blurred as she sucked the breath from his lungs. Automatically he began to push her over on to the couch, and then he remembered that it was already occupied.

'Stop!' he gasped, recovering his balance and pulling them away from Shitski's body. 'Not with him here.'

'We could go to your dressing room.'

He was a little surprised at her, to say the least.

'That's not the point . . .' He hesitated. The combination of sex and death was disturbing his equilibrium. 'We've got to get rid of the evidence.'

'You mean Sergei?'

'We've got to get him out of here.'

'And then what?'

'We've got to—'

He was interrupted by a knocking on the door.

'Go away, Seymour!' he commanded, angrily.

'Er, sorry, is Natasha there?' a woman's voice enquired nervously.

'It's my dresser,' Natasha confided to Philip. She went closer to the door. 'Yes, Jenny?'

'I've got your costume. Can I come in?'

Natasha looked at her watch.

'It'll be the half in ten minutes,' she said to Philip. 'I can't keep her out for long.'

'Stall her.'

She picked the dressing-room key off the table and unlocked the door.

'Jenny,' she said quietly, keeping the door crack narrow. 'Sergei's having a nap in the corner. He's very tired and I don't want to disturb him, but Philip has very kindly offered me the use of his dressing room. Would you mind taking the costume over the other side and I'll join you in a minute?'

She closed and relocked the door. Philip appraised her coolly.

'Well done.'

She had dealt with the dresser confidently; she appeared to be in command. But then, she was a damned good actress. If she could only keep it up, they might just get away with it.

'We haven't got time to get rid of him now,' he said, indicating the corpse. 'We'll have to do it after the show. I've got the only other key.'

He patted his pocket. She was already sorting through her make-up, picking out what she needed.

'I'll go and get my stuff,' he said. 'I'll start getting ready in here, and then, when you're done, we can swap over. It'll look a bit peculiar, but that can't be helped. Of course, there's nothing we can do when we're both on stage, but that can't be helped either. Have you got your car here, by the way?'

'Yes.'

'Good. See you in a minute.'

He took the passkey out of his pocket. She laid a hand on his sleeve.

'Have you got a pen?'

'Yes. Why?'

'I might as well start on my first-night cards. While I'm waiting.'

'Of course . . .'

He gave her his pen casually. He was trying not to stare. Was she acting now, or was she really in control? The more he looked at her, the more mysterious she became.

'Do you want yours now?' she asked, taking a card out of an envelope on the desk. It was a photograph of Henry Irving from the National Portrait Gallery. He had been planning to give her his favourite Ellen Terry from the same collection.

'Thanks ... If I forget to say it later, good luck tonight.'

'And to you.'

'Act as if your life depends on it.'

'It does.'

They were a well-matched pair, he decided, as he left her dressing room and walked on down the corridor: the Irving and Terry of theatrical homicide.

'Guinness with a raspberry top, I said. Yes, that's right, and a port and lemon.'

The old actor sounded hoarse and exasperated. The foyer was packed and it had taken much too long to get the barman's attention. It was unpleasantly hot and sticky. He carried the drinks with difficulty through the press, spilling beer all over his fingers.

'Nowhere to sit, I suppose?' he enquired grumpily, offering the port and lemon to his friend.

'Fat chance,' said Seymour, who was in a very jolly mood. 'Come on! You haven't even told me I was wonderful yet.'

'You were wonderful yet.'

'Ah! Is it not passing brave to be a queen and ride in triumph through South Hammersmith? Do you mean it?'

'Yes.'

'Seriously?'

'Yes.'

'How seriously?'

'Seymour, you can't demand a compliment and then keep trying to make me retract it. I think you were very good. The whole thing, much to my surprise after what you told me, was very good. I do mean it.'

'The whole thing?'

'All right, I hated the set. That ridiculous Ford Cortina stuck bang in the middle upstage was perhaps the most ridiculous thing I have ever seen in a theatre, but apart from that I liked it very much. Who are all these bloody people anyway?'

'Oh, you know, typical first-night crowd. Difficult to tell, of course, but seems like they enjoyed it.'

'I think they did. Really, Seymour, all that palaver you were giving me about what a disaster it was going to be – you didn't half lay it on with a trowel!'

'I meant it! Honest!'

'But you said Natasha was dull, insipid and lifeless. Nothing could have been further from the truth!'

'I know, I know, but . . . all I can say is I'm as surprised as you are, only more so. Quite stunned, in fact.'

'Where is she, by the way? I haven't seen her.'

Seymour glanced into the mass of bodies filling the space between them and the bar. He shrugged.

'Don't know. Maybe she hasn't come out yet. She was good, wasn't she?'

'Good? She was electric.'

'I know. It was extraordinary enough being out there on stage with her. The footlights must have been crackling.'

'This is the Riverside Studios, dear, there aren't any footlights.'

'Don't be pedantic, you know what I mean.'

'I do, and I agree with you. It's one of the most passionate, vibrant Shakespearian performances I've ever seen. The audience was thrilled.'

'So were we all. We were crammed into the wings all the way through, didn't dare take our eyes off the stage. You wouldn't have got a million to one on that happening half an hour before the performance.'

'Stop exaggerating.'

'I'm not! Really! I swear to you by all I hold dear, by my signed portrait of Noel and my lifetime friendship with Dorothy, that not once in the entire rehearsal period did Natasha's performance rise above the level of pallid mediocrity. Honestly, it was unenergized, unimaginative and utterly frightfully fearfully uninspiring to the nth degree, and if I so much as exaggerate by a *soupçon* of a hair's breadth you can knock me sideways with your wand right here and now!'

'I still find it hard to believe you.'

'Get thee behind me! I'm telling you, Natasha's transformation tonight was nothing short of miraculous. God knows how she did it, something must have just clicked. There was so much intensity coming from her I hardly dared look. It was an ugly duckling turning into a swan. Doctor Theatre effecting a wonder cure.'

'She's not ill, is she?'

'It was Doctor Theatre the psychiatrist. The woman was on the verge of a nervous breakdown. And when she found Shitski in flag del with that Arts tart from the Beeb I thought she was going to have the mother of all crack-ups; she could have gone either way, you know. I genuinely didn't think we'd be going on tonight, she was in such a state, and who could blame her? The smell of the greasepaint, the roar of the crowd, must have galvanized her out of it.'

'The smell of this crowd is going to galvanize me in a moment, I can tell you. Don't these people ever wash?'

'You're talking about my public. Show a little respect. Did you like my costume?'

'The business-suit look rather flatters you, actually. Gives you a refined and distinguished air. I scarcely recognized you.'

'Romans are meant to be bureaucrats, you see. I think Shitski sees Octavius as a kind of Jacques Delors figure.'

'Where do directors get their ideas from? Where is he, by the way?'

'Who?'

'Shitski, of course. Who did you think I meant, Jacques Delors?'

'I don't think he could make it.'

'You surprise me.'

'I haven't a clue where Shitski is. Probably doesn't dare show his face after the way Natasha sorted him out.'

'You were saying. So the worm turned, did it?'

'Under extreme provocation. Shitski's probably off sulking somewhere. He usually is. Besides, everyone here looks like they're having a good time. I don't think he can bear to be in the company of people having a good time. Still, I expect he'll take the credit in the morning.'

'I think the critics loved it.'

'Do you? Really?'

'I was sitting almost behind two of them. The odd-looking

one with the beard and the dwarf with dandruff. Scribbling away furiously, seemed enthusiastic. Most unusual. I reckon they adored Natasha.'

'What about me?'

'How could anyone possibly adore you? Don't be absurd.'

'You say the cruellest things, and I love you for it dearly. What did you think of Philip?'

'Ah, my lookalike. Very good.'

'You don't sound wildly keen.'

'What's wrong with "very good", Seymour? I'd be delighted if someone described a performance of mine as "very good".'

'Dream on, dear . . . I hope the critics are rather more forthcoming. Philip likes to be the best, you see.'

'He wasn't. But he was very good. Where is he, by the way?'

'You keep asking me where everybody is. How should I know?'

'But I can't see any of them. Natasha, Fletcher, Shitski . . . why aren't they all here basking in the acclaim? I know I would be.'

'Perhaps they don't like parties.'

'I'd have thought someone with Fletcher's ego would be right in there lapping it up.'

'Perhaps he's miffed at not being the best. How does he compare with Dick Jones?'

'Not at all badly.'

'That's a relief. I wouldn't have liked to be in Jones's shoes if Philip had bombed. Philip might have got very nasty.'

'How nasty?'

'I think, between you and me, that he probably would have murdered him. Now come on, I don't intend to stand here in the corner all night with you when my drink's in urgent need of a refill. Oh look, it's Natasha, she's here at last. Come on, old friend, you can tell her how wonderful you thought she was. I don't suppose she'll object . . .'

## 12

Philip managed to leave his last cigarette for twenty-seven minutes. He was counting every second. He was cross with himself for not having bought another packet.

He heard footsteps down the corridor. He stopped in the act of lighting the cigarette, held his breath and listened. He had to drop the match suddenly when the flame began to tease his fingertip. The footsteps receded.

'Come on, Natasha, where are you?'

He had been sitting alone in her dressing room for nearly an hour. Alone, that was, if he discounted the dead body in the corner, which, on sound Cartesian principles, he was prepared to do.

'One of us has got to go out front,' he had said to her, after curtain down. 'It'll look suspicious if we're both not there; it had better be you.'

Better her, he had reasoned, because he was rather more experienced at body-sitting. He still didn't know how she was going to measure up, but what choice did he have? She'd coped well enough on stage; if she could handle it in the lions' den, the rest would be playing with pussycats. He couldn't think why he'd forgotten to ask her to get him some cigarettes.

He took a careful drag; he was trying to make it last. Adrenaline had got him thus far through the night, pumping urgency into his brain and not giving space for uncomfortable thoughts to settle. Now backstage was empty he found the silence disquieting, and his nerves were on the limit. Nor did it help that he was feeling exhausted. The performance on its own could have been expected to tire him; the strain of the dressing-room sub-plot had completely worn him out. He hadn't had a moment to himself all night; every second he was offstage he'd been on guard duty. He wanted to be out having a drink, relaxing, soaking up the praise which he so richly deserved, not minding a dead Russian. It wasn't as if he was even responsible. Where the hell was Natasha? He was getting irritated with her.

'She was bloody good, though,' he murmured appreciatively, and then, casting a dark glance in the direction of her former paramour: 'No thanks to you . . .'

It was odd, but the presence of Shitski's corpse was making him feel squeamish. He didn't know why, he was used to bodies. Fear was in the mind, inert flesh was not innately frightening. Not to him, anyway. Not to cool-blooded Philip, with ice for a heart and mercury in his veins.

Reluctantly he finished the cigarette and put it out. He was trembling ever so slightly. He tried not to notice. He looked into the mirror over the dressing-room table, which was studded with light bulbs. His hair seemed to glow.

'I'd just like to say that I thought you were bloody marvellous tonight,' he said, and was pleased to hear that at least he sounded calm.

'Why, thank you,' he answered modestly. 'It was all a bit touch and go, of course. At one point I seriously thought we might be staring disaster in the face.'

'Surely not! You must have been gratified by the notices the next day.'

'Naturally one is pleased when one's modest efforts attract favourable critical attention.'

'But the comparisons with Olivier at his best! Don't you find all the praise a little embarrassing?'

'No.'

'Were you surprised at winning the *Evening Standard* Best Actor award?'

'Not as surprised as Dick Jones.'

'How did your rival take your enormous success?'

'Badly.'

'He wasn't even nominated, was he?'

'Unfortunately they don't have a Best Amateur category.'

'Wasn't he nominated for something else?'

'Only Slimiest Welsh Shitbag. Won it hands down.'

'Philip, are you in there?'

He jumped. He had been lolling casually on the edge of the table, talking to different profiles as he spotted them in the variously angled mirrors. Natasha's voice almost made him fall off.

'Where have you been?' he hissed, slipping off the catch and letting her in. She breezed past him in a champagne haze.

'I'm sorry, they just wouldn't let me go!' she announced, flopping into the nearest chair and reaching for her handbag. She leant towards the mirror and began reapplying lipstick. 'They're asking everyone to leave by the way, I think they're going on to Seymour's. I said you had a headache and were resting, like you told me. They made me promise to try to drag you along. Who were you talking to just now?'

'No one.'

'I thought I heard voices.'

'I was thinking aloud.'

'Watch out, dear, or it'll be the funny farm for you!'

She giggled and smudged her chin. He watched suspiciously as she searched in her bag for a tissue.

'How many drinks have you had?'

'Just one or two. I don't know, Philip, people kept pressing glasses into my hand. Everyone loved it, you know. I'm sorry, I should have brought something back for you.'

'Nice of you to remember,' he said caustically. 'Do you also remember why you went out there in the first place? Or do I have to remind you that while you've been gallivanting I've been stuck here minding a dead body, cause of death not entirely unattributable to someone in this very room and it doesn't happen to be me?'

Philip had to sit down again. The trembling had intensified and it was worst in his legs; his knees were knocking together. He ached for a cigarette.

'Philip, don't be so mean!'

She threw down her lipstick and tissue and, as he sat, jumped up defiantly. She was shaking, too.

'It was you who told me to go out there,' she snapped, and

there was no tipsiness in her voice now. 'You who told me to act up, and that's what I did. Terror got me through tonight, sheer liquid terror. Every moment I was out there I was imagining that – that thing lying there in the corner. I knew that at any moment someone was going to come in and find him, and I'd heard what you said, I understood that as soon as they did, that was it, curtains for me, and the rest of my life behind bars. And I wouldn't have stuck it, Philip, oh no. I'd have got another cyanide tablet from somewhere. And then I got thinking, and the more I thought, the more it came down to if it was between me and – that thing – then it was going to be me, me, me; every time. If anyone thinks I'm going to let that bastard screw up my life just because he's dead they can start thinking again. I was bloody enjoying myself out there, I loved every second of it, for the first time in years I felt as if I was free, just released from prison rather than facing the prospect of being thrown into one, and if I had a couple of drinks so bloody what, and don't you ever dare lecture me again, Philip Fletcher, because I've had it up to here with being pushed around and you can look at what happened to the last bastard who tried.'

She marched angrily over to the couch and stared down at the immobile lump under the camel blanket.

'I know what I've done, Philip . . .' Her voice was filled with passionate intensity, but controlled. He watched her admiringly. It wasn't every day he had the privilege of witnessing a private benefit performance from an indubitably first-rate actress. 'All right, I admit it, I stayed out there and I had a drink too many because I didn't want to come back here and face this – thing. I couldn't forget, of course, but I could pretend. We're in a theatre, aren't we? Suspension of disbelief, isn't that what it's all about? But, as you say, I have to learn to live with the consequences of my actions.'

She bent down, took the corner of the blanket and pulled it off smoothly, like a conjuror revealing a trick disappearance. Only without the disappearance.

'There. That wasn't so bad, was it?'

She sounded quite pleased with herself. Philip was fascinated. He had thought of himself as being perhaps unique. It had not occurred to him that anyone else, still less a woman, could have reacted with quite such cool detachment to the fact of murder.

'Well?' she demanded, turning away imperiously from the corpse, and seeming, by that gesture, to dismiss it as a matter of any importance. 'What's it going to be?'

'Sorry?'

'You said you'd think of a way of getting rid of this bastard. What have you come up with?'

'Suicide.'

'What?'

'He killed himself.'

'Philip, I wasn't asking for a definition, I know what suicide means. I was expressing astonishment at your suggestion. It's ludicrous.'

'I wasn't proposing we leave him to be discovered here. We've got to get him out of the theatre. The last time anyone saw him alive was when you and he were in here together. Then you told your dresser he was having a nap. We'll both say we saw him leave just after the half, about twenty minutes later. No one will back us up on that, but so what? It's not going to occur to anyone that you might have killed him – why should it? We'll get the body down to the river and dump it over the towpath. I know the place, the other side of the bridge by the Harrods depository. He took the tablet, then slipped gracefully into the water. With any luck the body won't be found for a few days. Meantime we'll just act puzzled at his mysterious disappearance, like everyone else, and when they discover him you can put in a lot of wailing and gnashing. Tell the police he was a suicidal depressive, I'll back you up.'

'Are you serious?'

'Of course!'

'You mean you've been in here thinking about it for the last hour and that's the best you can come up with. It's pathetic!'

'I admit it's not perfect, but what else can we do? When they do the autopsy they'll find the cyanide. Once they do that, it's natural for them to think of suicide, we'll just be prompting them.'

'But you told that bitch about the cyanide!'

'You'll have to deny it, you can't admit to walking around with poisonous substances on you. The police may suspect, they could even give you a serious grilling, but they won't be able to pin anything on you. There's no evidence, only hearsay.'

'I don't believe this. I seriously do not believe this . . .'

She sat down heavily on the arm of the couch. Shitski's toe must have been sticking into her, for, with an irritated shrug, she pushed his foot away.

'Let me get this straight, Philip. You want us to pretend that this bastard walked out of here after having had the flaming row to end all flaming rows with me, marched over Hammersmith Bridge, took a suicide pill and conveniently fell into the river. Are you mad?'

'As I said, it's not perfect—'

'Not perfect? It's idiotic!'

'Natasha, what do you suggest?'

'I don't know . . .' She gestured helplessly. 'Can't we dispose of him in an acid bath or something?'

Philip's fascination turned momentarily to awe. For the first time in years he was genuinely shocked. She was clearly capable of going further than him.

'I cannot imagine that it would be easy to acquire sufficient quantities of acid innocently,' he said, with care. 'Nor would I feel comfortable performing such an operation in my bath.'

'We could use mine,' she answered matter-of-factly.

'That's not the point,' said Philip, who doubted that he would ever again be able to play happily with his rubber ducks. 'You don't just go and buy ten gallons of acid over the counter at Boots, you know. And we can't go lugging the body around like Polonius. We've got to get rid of it.'

'Can't we bury it in a disused quarry somewhere?'

'Do I look like the kind of man who'd know where we could find a disused quarry? Besides, buried bodies have a habit of being dug up by members of the canine fraternity, and if there's even a one percent chance of that happening we can't afford to take it, because then they're going to know for sure it's murder, aren't they? No, we've got to be bold, and it's precisely because the idea of suicide is so preposterous that it's going to work. Why should they believe he killed himself? It's a good question, but ask yourself this one: if they find his body in a few days floating in the Thames with cyanide in his bloodstream, by what means are they going to leap to the conclusion that you were responsible? Put yourself in the police's shoes. If they find any body, Shitski's or anyone's, in the circumstances I've just described, they're obviously going to think it's a suicide. Why should it occur to them to begin a murder investigation? Maybe they'll talk to Melissa and she'll tell them about the cyanide. And who told her? Me. And what will I say? I'll deny ever telling her anything of the sort. Who's the better actor, me or Melissa? It'll look like malicious invention on her part. You must learn to play to your strengths, Natasha, and in our cases these do not include quarry hunting and acid bathing. We'll concoct stories about Shitski's latent suicidal depression and you will spin them brilliantly. We will bluff and we will lie, or, to put it another way, we shall act our way out of this mess. Now, what say we get on with the unsavoury bit and remove our Polonius to the nearest willow aslant a brook? I'm tired and I want to go to bed.'

'I had a little drink about an hour ago . . .'

Natasha sat thoughtfully on the arm of the couch, humming the tune. After a few moments she nodded.

'All right . . . I still don't like it, but I see your point. How do we get him out of here?'

'You bring your car round to River Terrace. Is there space in the boot?'

'Yes.'

'I'll wait till the theatre's locked up, then I'll bring him out the Studio side exit. That'll be the risky time, but there's no other way.'

'Will you be able to carry him?'

'If I can't I'll put him in a costume skip.'

'That'll be awkward.'

'I'll try to carry him.'

'He's heavy.'

'I'll manage. Park the car as near as possible to the door.'

'Philip?'

'Yes.'

'Are you scared?'

'A little.'

'You seem awfully good at all this.'

'I have hidden talents.'

'I know. I never guessed.'

'That's why they're hidden.'

'I'll never be able to repay you.'

'If you could get me some cigarettes I'd consider myself paid in full.'

'I have twenty Marlboro in my handbag.'

'You don't smoke.'

'I thought I might start again. It's nineteen Marlboro, actually. I don't think I will. It's bad for pregnant women.'

'As one-track minds go yours is strikingly unitary.'

'Here are the cigarettes.'

'Thanks. You may have saved my life. You'd better get going.'

'Can I have a kiss first?'

'Only if I can.'

It was more of a clinging, less of a passionate embrace than before. She held on to him for a long time; she seemed as reluctant as he was to let go, and he found this hint of vulnerability comforting: she had seemed so much in control it was unreal. Where did the actor stop and the person begin? He wasn't even sure on his own account. One thing was for sure – it had been a hell of a performance so far.

Eventually they parted. He checked the corridor for her and she went without another word. He locked the door and put the catch on for extra assurance. Then he turned off the lights and felt his way back to his chair.

He took out a Marlboro and read his watch by the match flame. It was gone half past eleven. Natasha had said that they'd been asked to leave, but it might take anything up to half an hour to clear the theatre. In any case, he would have to give it longer than that. He sat quietly and smoked.

He heard loud-spirited voices outside. He recognized some of them. A dressing-room door slammed and the noise receded. He put out his cigarette and stared into the darkness. He lit another.

The flare of the match outlined Shitski's body. It would be cold by now. He imagined picking it up, a weight of dead meat. While polluting his lungs with tar he tried to steady his breath. He finished the cigarette and counted in his head, slowly. When he had reached a hundred he struck a match and looked at his watch. It was only ten to twelve.

More footsteps approached. He flicked out the match and sat very still. The footsteps stopped outside the door. There was a light knocking.

'Sergei?' whispered Melissa Pine. 'Sergei, are you in there?'

In a manner of speaking, replied Philip in his head. He concentrated on attaining the perfect immobility of an artist's model.

'Sergei!' Melissa's voice was slurred. She knocked impatiently on the door again. 'Where are you, Sergei?'

Another set of footsteps approached from the opposite direction.

'I'm sorry, miss, we're closing up here now,' said the company stage manager.

'I'm from the BBC,' declared Melissa, in much the way Ali Baba might have exclaimed 'Open Sesame'.

'Well, I'm sure Jim'll fix it for you to come back tomorrow. We're locking up.'

'Have you seen Sergei?'

'He was out front, wasn't he?'

'When?'

'I don't know ... Good night, now.'

Philip heard her footsteps pattering away rapidly down the corridor. He listened as the CSM tried all the dressing rooms in turn, confirming that they were locked. When he had finished his rounds, he retreated the way he had come.

Philip took out another Marlboro. Quite what the justification had been for claiming that Shitski might be 'out front' was beyond him, but, as with witnesses to a road accident, he had no doubt that any number of confusing testimonies would arise shortly to obscure police inquiries. He wondered if he could get away with claiming to have seen Shustikov himself, stalking about backstage in a manic depressive sulk. He had told bigger whoppers than that to the forces of law and order in his time. He lit the cigarette.

'It's just you and me,' he murmured in the direction of the invisible corpse. 'You randy bastard.'

He wondered how long Shitski had been carrying on with Melissa. She was so starstruck she couldn't have been a difficult conquest. Knowing his despotic nature, he would no doubt have considered the attentions of any available handmaidens as no more than his due.

Time passed. He chain-smoked and didn't enjoy the taste of any of them, but his nerves demanded massaging. Eventually he could stand the fetid atmosphere – and the waiting – no longer. He crept outside to reconnoitre.

The silence was comforting. He felt his way down the corridor to the side exit. He lit a match to check that the area was clear and noticed in the corner a portable hand trolley, of the kind used for shifting heavy boxes. There were some bungee straps hooked on to the handle, and it occurred to him that it might also have its uses in the disposal of heavy corpses. He wheeled the trolley back to the dressing room.

He risked turning on the light. It was gone half twelve and he had to be able to see what he was doing. He laid the trolley down next to the couch.

He took hold of Shitski under the armpits and pulled him on to the floor. It was the heaviest dead body he had ever fielded. He was glad that he had found the trolley. There was no way he could have carried him for more than a few paces.

He placed the feet on the plate at the bottom of the trolley, then straightened the body out by pulling on the wrists. The flesh was clammy to the touch, but now that he was active again it didn't bother him. He was in his element. Mr Burke with an Equity card.

He secured Shitski's body round the waist with the two longest bungees and, with the others, clipped the ankles to the bottom plate. It didn't look like enough, so he unfurled the camel blanket, ran one end under the back of the trolley and tied it to the other end over Shitski's chest, making a big crude knot which he pulled together as tightly as he could. He grasped the two rubber handles at the back and heaved the trolley upright.

The knees buckled and the body sagged, but the bindings were sufficient to keep it up. Philip turned the light off, backed the trolley out of the door, then locked it.

He proceeded cautiously down the corridor in the pitch darkness. The door at the end caused some difficulty, but he propped it open with a couple of stage weights and reversed his way through. He lit another match to get his bearings. A low and very convenient ramp led up to the exit. He slipped the bar, opened the door carefully and peered outside.

It was a cool dark night. He could only just make out Natasha in her car, though she was no more than a few yards away. He retrieved the stage weights, jammed the door open and slipped outside. He tapped gently on her window.

'You gave me a shock!' she whispered, winding it down. 'I didn't see you coming.'

'Then no one else has . . .'

He tiptoed to the corner and shot a quick glance each way along Crisp Road. The Riverside may not have boasted the most glamorous of locations, but it was better situated than most for the removal of inconvenient criminal evidence. He reflected that had she decided to murder Shitski backstage at the Haymarket or the Prince of Wales, then their predicament might have been much worse.

'Looks all clear,' he observed on his return.

'They've only just gone,' said Natasha. 'It took ages to clear them from the bar, then some of them were standing back there on the pavement chatting for ages. I think they were hoping to cadge a lift off me to Seymour's.'

'Did they ask why you were there?'

'I said I was waiting to see if Sergei turned up. That got

rid of them. I said I hadn't seen him since before the half and I was worried.'

'You can stop worrying now: he's turned up. Is the back door unlocked?'

'Aren't you going to put him in the boot?'

Philip shook his head.

'He's heavier than he looks. We'll lay him across the back seat and cover him with the blanket. We're only going over the bridge.'

'Couldn't we just tip him over when we're halfway across?'

'No water in his lungs. Wouldn't work.'

'Philip, how do you know all these things?'

'Shrewd guesswork . . . Get into the back seat and be ready for me. I'll need a hand.'

He checked once more that the street was deserted, then slipped back into the theatre. He levered the trolley away from the wall against which he had leant it, lifted the brake and lined up the wheels in the direction of the ramp. He could hear Natasha opening the rear passenger door.

He dropped down the rubber handles and pushed. It took a big heave to bounce it up over the lip of the exit, but once on the pavement it quickly picked up momentum. He had to pull back hard to bring the trolley to a halt.

He took the weight against his own body. He bent over the lolling head and felt for the knot around the chest.

'There are bungees round his ankles,' he whispered. 'Take them off!'

Natasha leant across the back seat and unclipped the elastic straps. Philip was struggling with the knot. Either he had tied it too enthusiastically, or the pressure of the body had tightened it. His fingers ached as he tried to prise the ends free.

He heard a noise to his right. He ignored it and carried on trying to dig his nails into the material. The noise was repeated, and this time he made it out. It was a muffled footstep, a sole scraping over the pavement. He froze.

'Sergei?'

A glacier began descending between Philip's shoulder blades. He turned his head round slowly.

'Sergei . . . talk to me!'

There was a sob in Melissa Pine's voice. She was coming towards them from the corner of the street, swaying unsteadily.

'Go away!' said Philip feebly, wondering where the hell she'd come from. 'He can't talk to you now!'

The car door on the other side slammed. Natasha came bounding on to the pavement.

'How dare you?' she demanded, or at least that was what Philip thought she was demanding – her voice was quivering so much it was hard to tell.

'Leave us alone!' he muttered despairingly, his own voice shaking just as much. 'Haven't you done enough damage?'

'I've got to talk to him!' Melissa whined drunkenly. 'You can't treat me like this, I'm from the BBC!'

Philip staggered as she grabbed his shoulder. He saw the blur of Natasha's hand and heard the smack of it hitting Melissa's cheek. Melissa yelped, but didn't let him go. Philip tried to lean forward, but Shitski's weight pressed him back again. He lost his balance and fell to the pavement.

He couldn't breathe. One of the handles was jammed into his stomach. The back of Shitski's head was pressing into his windpipe.

'Sergei?' said Melissa uncertainly.

Philip heaved with all his strength and the trolley tipped on to its side. Shitski's head thwacked the pavement. The light from the car interior spilled across the lifeless blur of his face.

'My God!' Melissa gasped. 'He's dead!'

'Don't exaggerate!' Philip gasped back, wondering why he was bothering. 'He's just not feeling very well . . .'

Philip squeezed himself out from under the trolley. Melissa covered her face with her hands and staggered backwards.

'You've murdered him! Murderers! Killers! Oh God! Oh no!'

She tried to scream, but could only manage a near voiceless hysterical whistle. She gave another drunken lurch to the side, then turned clumsily and ran away round the corner as fast as her clumpy heels would let her. Philip crawled up on to his knees.

'Natasha, where are you going?'

She had taken a couple of steps in Melissa's direction. She turned to him frantically.

'We can't let her get away! We'll have to kill her!'

'Don't be absurd!' Philip climbed painfully to his feet, feeling as much dazed by Natasha's sudden propensity for serial murder as by the latest catastrophic turn of events. 'We've already got one body on our hands. Help me get him up! Quick!'

They both bent down and hauled up the trolley by the handles. Unrestrained at the ankles, Shitski's legs were splayed all over the place. Natasha grabbed frantically at the camel knot.

'What are you doing?' Philip hissed.

'What do you mean? We've got to get him to the river!'

'Not now!'

He grabbed both handles and yanked the trolley away from her.

'For Christ's sake, Natasha! It won't work now. We've been rumbled!'

They stood for an awful frozen moment facing each other, both panting horribly for breath and trying to control their terror and despair.

'What are we going to do?' she whispered faintly.

Whatever it was, it couldn't involve standing there on the pavement for much longer. He imagined Melissa staggering across Hammersmith Broadway, frantically searching for a policeman. Of course, you could never find one when you wanted one, but that practically guaranteed she'd be back in five minutes with at least a dozen.

'Wait here!' he commanded, heaving up the trolley and dragging it back towards the theatre.

'Philip, where are you going?'

'How should I know? I'm improvising!'

He stumbled through the door and shot down the ramp so fast he almost had a major collision with the wall. He lit a match, took his bearings, and replaced the stage weights against the inner door. He pushed the trolley on into the corridor.

Behind him the exit was banged shut by the wind. The loud clanging noise had the finality of a cell door closing.

# 13

Sunlight, by degrees, began to fill the room. Philip lay in bed watching it creep across the ceiling. It was bright for a March morning.

He had the radio on, faintly, in the background. Between uneasy dozings he had listened to *Farming Today*, all of Naughtie and Humphreys, the nine o'clock news. Another bulletin was due in half an hour. So far there had been no references to dead Russian theatre directors.

He pushed away the covers and rose. He hadn't slept much, he felt exhausted. He went into the bathroom and examined his pale face in the mirror.

'The body is with the king, but the king is not with the body . . .'

That was one way of looking at it. He went to the kitchen to make coffee and thought of others. There was a part of his brain reserved for the hatching of schemes. It was empty this morning. The phone rang.

'The police have just left,' said Natasha down the line.

Philip sat on the arm of the sofa and tried to ignore the lump coagulating in his throat. The ringing phone had sent his pulse into overdrive. He didn't know how to control his fear.

'What did you tell them?' he asked.

'What you said. I told them I'd driven home and Sergei went off with you for another drink. I said I hadn't seen or heard from him since. I gave them your address.'

'Good. Well done.'

She sounded calm. Why had he been so anxious to take all the responsibility on to himself? She seemed to be coping better than he was.

'What about Melissa?' he asked.

'I said she was raving drunk. Sergei didn't want to talk to her; we had a fight; she ran off; she was hysterical.'

'And the police?'

'Seemed to agree. She still is hysterical, apparently.'

'Good. Did you sleep?'

'Not much. You?'

'No.'

'I wish you'd been here.'

'Yes.'

'I wanted you last night, Philip.'

'I wanted you too.'

He had spent half the night thinking about her, desiring her. The other half he had spent thinking about her dead lover. Sex and death sharing the billing; his own version of *The Odd Couple*. She had wanted him to stay with her and he had wanted to as well, desperately, but it had been out of the question. She had dropped him off, discreetly, at about 1.30 a.m., and driven on home alone.

'They'll be back,' he warned her. 'When Sergei doesn't turn up.'

'They asked me to get him to call them.'

'They'll be lucky.'

Not as lucky as they needed to be, though. The phone was damp with his sweat. Where was his legendary coolness now that he needed it?

'Philip, what are we going to do?'

'It'll be all right, don't worry . . .' ('Don't worry!' he repeated to himself. Who was he trying to kid?) 'I've had a few thoughts.'

'Like what?'

Like none at all, was the honest answer. He stalled: 'Let's not discuss it over the phone. In fact, from now on let's not discuss anything over the phone. It's paranoia, I know, but we might get a crossed line, and you know what surveillance devices they have these days.'

'Call me Squidgy.'

'Precisely. Let's meet at the theatre. Midday. Don't want

to be too early, it'll look odd. If anyone asks, say we want to go over a few lines together.'

He put the phone down and went to run a bath. He lay in it with the water up to his chin, eyes closed, thinking. Maybe, when he'd finished, he'd have to see about refilling it with acid after all. When he had had that little thought, he ceased to enjoy his bath and he got out. He stood on the mat, staring uneasily into his misted reflection in the mirror.

'Mirror, mirror, on the wall, who's the cleverest of them all?'

'You are.'

'Then why can't I think of anything?'

It had never been a problem before, disposing of bodies. In the past he'd just left them where he'd found them. That was not an option in the present case.

'They're not going to believe suicide now, not after Melissa. If we hide the body and it turns up they'll know it's murder. We've got to get rid of the evidence completely and at the same time prove that Melissa is lying. There's only one problem.'

'What's that?'

'She isn't.'

He got dressed and went back into the living room. The police would be round soon, the Rubicon had to be crossed. He stared carefully at the tight spiral staircase in the corner that led up to the first floor. He had bruised himself black and blue slipping up and down it during his alcoholic phases.

'I think I'd rather sleep on the sofa . . .' he murmured wisely to himself.

He got a sleeping bag out of the bedroom cupboard, unzipped it and threw it carelessly over the back of the sofa. He plumped up some cushions at one end, stood back and examined the effect critically. He fiddled pointlessly with the cushions, told himself he was wasting his time, but carried on fiddling. He sent himself into the kitchen to make more coffee. He wanted something stronger, a bad sign. He made do with caffeine and nicotine. While he smoked he arranged empty bottles and two dirty glasses on the floor by the sofa. He was just putting out his third cigarette when the door buzzer rang.

'Mr Philip Fletcher?' said the voice down the intercom. 'It's the police. Could I have a word, please, sir?'

'Yes, of course. First floor.'

He was a uniformed officer, mild in appearance and polite in manner. He introduced himself as Constable Wheeler.

'Not my neck of the woods up here, sir,' he said pleasantly. 'Took a while to find you. Miss Fielding gave me your address.'

'I know, she rang me.'

'She did?' The constable looked surprised, but also a little relieved. 'Ah well, sir, you know what it's about then. Do you know where I can find Mr, er . . .' he consulted his notebook, 'Mr Shistikov, if that's how you pronounce it.'

'Near enough. I'm afraid not, you must have just missed him . . .'

Philip wandered over loosely to the sofa. He gave the sleeping bag a casual tweak:

'He crashed out here last night. I haven't a clue what time he left this morning, I was well out of it myself. Must have been before ten, though.'

'Why ten, sir?'

'That was when Natasha rang. Woke me up. There was no sign of him then. Must have let himself out.'

'So he was here with you last night, was he, sir?'

'Yes. Not that we planned it that way. We were all going off to have a drink together, after the show, the three of us, then Natasha decided . . . well, I think she decided she was tired, she went home, Sergei stayed with me, we went looking for somewhere to get a drink, couldn't find anywhere, so I said come back to Highbury, I've got some booze, we had a few together, as you can see . . . well, by then it was too late to go home so I offered him the sofa, and that's the last I saw of him . . . He's probably on his way back home. At least let's hope so. He was in a funny mood last night: depressed, moody . . . I only pray he didn't sneak off to see that bloody silly Melissa girl.'

'Ah yes, sir . . .' The policeman cleared his throat uncomfortably. 'As you may know, Miss Pine has been making alle-gations.'

'Really, Constable?' Philip perched himself casually on the back of the sofa, taking the weight off his feet. He sounded relaxed and unflustered. He was pleased with his performance so far, though he knew that the key part of the scene was just coming: 'Natasha did say something about this, but I'm not sure I understood her properly. You'll have to forgive me, I'm afraid my brain's still a bit fogged up this morning – shouldn't have finished that last bottle with Sergei! What allegations?'

'She claims that the last time she saw you all together, Mr Shistikov was dead.'

Philip laughed indulgently. He toyed with a cigarette as he adopted a careless Rattiganesque air.

'Dead drunk, maybe. She wasn't in the best of nick herself, you know. In fact, I'd hazard a guess that she had as much alcohol in her veins last night as the rest of us put together.'

'You may well be right about that, sir,' answered the police-man wryly. 'She's been quite a handful.'

'For us too, Constable. Look, I didn't want to say anything, but you probably know anyway that there's been a bit of non-sense between her and Sergei. There's a lot of recrimination and argument flying around, it's not a healthy situation at all, probably why he's been in a bit of a mental state. When I said Natasha went home because she was tired, it was actually because she and Melissa had this flaming row in the street. That's when Sergei gave Melissa the brush-off and of course she didn't like it. I expect that's why the silly girl went over-board with her drinking last night, started imagining things.'

'And Mr Shistikov was perfectly all right when you last saw him, was he?'

'He'd had a few too many, yes. But he wasn't dead. Ha! If he was I'd like to know how he got out of my front door this morning! As I say, he's probably on his way home now even as we speak.'

'I'm sure he is, sir. I'm sorry to trouble you.'

'It's no trouble at all to me. It's such a bore for you. I know

Melissa's a bit barmy, but I didn't think she'd go this far off the rails. How is she, by the way?'

'She's under sedation. In hospital. Just routine. If you should hear anything from Mr Shistikov, I'd be grateful if you could get him to give us a ring at the station. I'll give you the number.'

'Thank you, Constable. He's very erratic, of course – Natasha says he sometimes goes walkabout for days.'

'Yes, she did tell me that.'

'She did? Oh well . . .' Philip shrugged. He was pleased that Natasha seemed to have remembered her lines. 'He'll turn up!'

'I hope so, sir. Miss Fielding was worried he might do himself an injury.'

'How do you mean?'

'Well, like you said, sir, apparently he was very depressed last night. He gets these black moods, you see.'

'Really?'

'Yes, almost suicidal, according to Miss Fielding. Still, as you say, I'm sure he'll turn up. Thank you for your time, sir, and, once again, sorry to bother you.'

'Not at all. Good day.'

Philip waited until the policeman had gone before lighting the cigarette he had been using for a prop. His hand was steady, as he had known from long experience it would be: no matter how bad his pre-performance nerves, once he got into the first scene he was always all right. The problem would come later, with the second act. And the problem with that was that it hadn't been written yet.

'Good show so far though,' he muttered encouragingly to himself. 'It'll be favourably received in the bar during the interval drinks . . .'

His voice slipped away in a breathy whisper. His jaw fell open as a sudden realization struck him. He slapped himself on the forehead with the heel of his hand.

'Bloody hell!' he gasped. 'The reviews!'

He grabbed for his coat and dashed out of the door. He scurried across the Fields to the newsagent's and bought each of the quality papers. He hailed a cab, spread himself across the back, and tore through the collected Arts pages.

His taxi arrived at the theatre half an hour later. He folded the papers under his arm, pulled up his collar and marched grimly through to backstage, grunting minimal hellos to the stage manager and his deputy. Natasha was in her dressing room.

'Am I glad to see you!' she declared, flinging her arms round him the moment the door was closed. She lifted her lips towards his. He turned away brusquely.

'Not now,' he muttered. He reached awkwardly into his pocket for a cigarette. One of the newspapers slipped out of the thick pile under his arm and fell to the floor. Natasha picked it up.

'You've got it open on the right page, at least,' she said with a little laugh. There was a large photograph of her at the top, holding her crown above her head for the 'Immortal longings' speech. All of the papers had photographs of her. There were none of him. He lit his cigarette.

'Some nice reviews, eh?' she offered, with what to Philip seemed an infuriatingly self-satisfied smile. He gritted his teeth.

'Nice?' he repeated. He glanced at the notice beneath the photograph. He read aloud: ' "Philip Fletcher's Antony, unfortunately, seems a dry pale creature in comparison with Miss Fielding's astonishing, supercharged Cleopatra . . ." Nice! Call that nice? What about this one?'

He threw down the paper and snatched up another:

' "Fletcher shines brightly enough at the beginning, but is soon overshadowed by Miss Fielding's blazing supernova of a performance . . ." I'm not sure I'd use "nice" to describe that. "Utter crap" maybe, but "nice", no. And what about this? The best of all! An afterthought tagged on at the end: "Philip Fletcher's Antony, though perhaps lacking inspiration, is in the final analysis adequate enough" . . . Ha!'

He hurled the whole stack of papers into the corner. He took a deep angry drag of his cigarette.

' "Adequate"! The most humiliating word in the critics'

lexicon. How dare they! Fucking talentless useless bunch of bastards. Wouldn't recognize great acting if it bit them in the balls. Not that they've got any.'

'Philip! Don't sulk. It's very unbecoming.'

'For Christ's sake, Natasha! You've been total rubbish all through rehearsals, you turn it on for one performance and the bastards are fawning all over you! I've sweated blood for this one, how do you think I feel?'

'I don't believe this! How can you be so petty?'

'You didn't even want to give the bloody performance. If it wasn't for me you'd be in the nick facing twenty years, and don't you forget it!'

'Why, you vain arrogant little shit!'

'That's as maybe, but I'm right and I'm very very pissed off. Is that OK with you?'

'Philip!' Natasha extended her arms towards him plaintively, then let them fall to her sides with a gesture of helpless despair. 'Philip, I think you're forgetting why we're here.'

'Humph . . .'

He sat down heavily on the dressing-room table. He puffed heavily on his cigarette, ignoring her eyes.

'Philip, what are we going to do with Sergei?'

Her voice was calm and measured. He sensed the effort it was costing her and was unable to suppress a burst of admiration. He mellowed.

'To be honest I haven't a bloody clue. We may have to burn the theatre down.'

'He's still here, then?'

'Yes.'

'Where?'

'Safe enough.'

'That's what you told me last night. What have you done with him, Philip?'

'You wouldn't want to know.'

'I don't dare not know. You've got to tell me.'

'You'll only worry.'

'I'll only worry!' she repeated incredulously. 'What the fuck do you think I'm doing now?'

She had a point. Philip thought about it for a moment while stubbing out his cigarette.

'All right,' he said. 'I'll show you. Come with me.'

He led her out of the dressing room, down the corridor and out through the foyer into the auditorium. The working lights were on, but there was no one about. He took her hand and guided her on to the set.

'Philip, what are we doing here?'

Her voice was very quiet and filled with suspicion. She stood back from him, in the sand on the centre forestage, as if to make sure he remained fully in view.

Philip walked carefully upstage, kicking aside the snowy drifts of tiny white polystyrene shavings. He stopped in front of the set designer's *pièce de résistance*, the derelict Ford Cortina. He tapped on the roof.

'He's in the boot.'

'What?' said Natasha, very faintly.

'In the boot. That's where I put him when I came back in last night. Only place I could think of.'

A beat. Natasha's voice swelled tremulously: 'Philip, are you mad!'

'Ssh! Keep your voice down, someone's coming . . .'

It was the stage manager, who signalled to Philip from the wings. Natasha, unable quite to dispel the incandescent shock in her eyes, had to turn away.

'Ah, Philip,' said the stage manager. 'Knew you were around.'

'Yes, we're just going through a few lines.'

'Ah, right. There's a copper here to see you. I told him to wait in your dressing room.'

'That's fine,' said Philip breezily. Out of the corner of his eye he noted Natasha's absolute stillness. 'Did he say what he wanted?'

The stage manager shook his head. Philip shrugged.

'I'm sure it's nothing important . . .' He glanced casually across at Natasha. 'I probably won't be a moment. Do you want to wait here?'

'No I do not,' she answered firmly. 'I think I'll wait somewhere else.'

She turned and marched offstage with an air of military determination. She did not look either at Philip or at the Ford Cortina. Philip went out at a more leisurely pace. He didn't read anything in particular into the police returning so quickly. They'd probably forgotten to ask him something, it was no doubt all perfectly trivial. Besides, he could handle the police.

'Why, hello again!' he said cheerily as he went into his dressing room, thinking that the pleasant young Constable Wheeler would be happy to make a joke of it. 'Long time no see . . .'

'It certainly is, Mr Fletcher,' said the square, ruggedly built man standing in the corner with hands clasped behind. 'A long time indeed.'

Philip stopped abruptly, half inside the door. This wasn't what he had been expecting at all. This was a quite different copper kettle of fish.

'Well, what a surprise,' he said at last, without exaggeration. He stepped inside the dressing room and closed the door behind him, fixing his unsmiling grizzled visitor with as unperturbed a glance as he was able to muster in the circumstances.

'And to what do I owe this honour – Inspector Higginbottom?'

# 14

'It's Superintendent, actually,' said the policeman with leaden humourlessness.

'Congratulations,' murmured Philip drily as he walked over to the dressing-room table, against which he carefully leant his weight. 'Have a seat.'

'I prefer to stand.'

'As you wish. It is a long time isn't it? Where was it? Bath, I presume.'

'Brighton.'

'Ah yes, of course. Brighton. You do get around. Still, quite a long way from home, aren't you?'

'Not as far as you might think, Mr Fletcher . . .'

There was a gleam in the policeman's big unblinking eyes which Philip didn't like the look of. Mind you, he thought, there wasn't much about the fellow he did like the look of: he had the jowly, squashed-nose mug of a B-movie heavy, the kind of face that attracts pockmarks like the moon entices asteroids, and where not even high-pressure sandblasting would have had much effect on the permanent fuzz of five o'clock shadow. It was unlikely that he would ever win a beauty contest.

'I've been transferred, actually. I'm back with the Metropolitan Police now.'

It was unlikely that he would ever win a poetry-reading competition either. His voice had the sinister nasally tone of a *Minder*-esque villain, or a Conservative MP.

'I see. And how are you finding life in the big city, Superintendent Higginbottom?'

'It's very interesting, Mr Fletcher, though I didn't come here to make small talk.'

'I didn't suppose that you had, Superintendent Higgin-bottom. You can't still be wanting to ask me questions about Richie Calvi, surely?'

'There are a number of questions I could think of asking about Richie Calvi, but I don't suppose I'd get very helpful answers.'

'What do you mean by that, Superintendent Higgin-bottom?'

'What I say, Mr Fletcher.'

'I have always endeavoured to cooperate as helpfully as possible with the forces of law and order, Superintendent Higginbottom.'

'Do you find something amusing about my name, Mr Fletcher?'

'I'm sorry?'

'It's the way you keep repeating it. The way you emphasize the last bit. A bit old to be making jokes about bottoms, aren't we, Mr Fletcher? Isn't that like something out of the school playground?'

'I see nothing extraordinary about your bottom, Superintendent. We all of us have one.'

'Trying to needle me, is it, Mr Fletcher? Fancy me as a foil for your legendary wit, eh?'

'Nothing personal, Superintendent, but I don't fancy you at all.'

'Very witty! Very very witty indeed!'

'I'm not sure I like your tone, Superintendent.'

'Oh don't you now? Well, that is a shame, isn't it? Oh no, please, Mr Fletcher, allow me!'

Philip stopped in the act of lighting his cigarette. Not that he had much choice in the matter: he had barely got the matches out of his pocket before the policeman, moving with considerably more litheness than his solid frame might suggest was possible, had pounced and singed the tip of his cigarette with a spurt from his disposable Bic. He repocketed the lighter and took a very small step back. Though he was the shorter man by a head, Philip found his close heavy presence every bit as intimidating as he was no doubt meant to find it. He took only the briefest of drags before letting his cigarette hand fall to his side. It had trembled.

'You seem nervous, Mr Fletcher.'

'I think you've been watching too many episodes of *Inspector Morse*, Superintendent.'

'Not quite my cup of tea, Mr Fletcher. I'm not much into the acting myself, you see. Real life's more my line. Real life and, you might say, real death. Where's Sergei Shustikov?'

The name skipped off his tongue with none of the syllabic fumbling shown by the hapless Constable Wheeler. An expert fluent delivery, it popped out like a googly, then pitched up and smacked Philip in the face with the force of a Malcolm Marshall bouncer.

'I, I haven't a clue,' he semi-stuttered, suddenly and horribly aware of the sweat bucketing off him, and the ice forming in his marrow.

'You'll have to do better than that. Where is he?'

'How the hell should I know?'

'You were with him weren't you? He was at your place last night. That's what you told the lad, isn't it? I've seen his notebook. Where's Shustikov?'

'I said I don't know—'

'I think you do, Mr Fletcher, I think you know perfectly well. He's dead, isn't he?'

'What? Huh . . . don't be absurd!'

'I've a witness says he was dead last night. Stone dead and you were with him. What have you done with the body?'

'I . . .'

For a moment Philip thought he was going to lose it: a wave of giddiness had swept over him, leaving him swamped in a bog of incoherence. As in a movie dream sequence, his eyes frosted out of focus, while voices jabbered meaninglessly in his head. He'd been punched in the mental solar plexus and he was reeling. He hung on, just, and regained his poise.

'What's your problem, Superintendent?' he demanded coolly, giving the policeman his most hostile slit-eyed glare.

'My problem, Mr Fletcher? The only problem I'm interested in solving is the disappearance of Mr—'

'No, no, Superintendent, I mean *your* problem . . .' Philip jabbed his finger at him emphatically. The space between them was so narrow that the policeman flinched. Philip pressed his advantage: 'I mean your problem with me, Superintendent Higg-in-bottom . . . What is it you don't like about me? Is it my face, my voice, my profession, or just the way I don't kowtow to you or respond to your insolent supercilious manner?'

'Watch it, Fletcher!'

'Mr Fletcher to you. What are you playing at, Superintendent, what are you trying to prove? This hasn't got anything to do with Sergei Shustikov, has it? Not even with Richie Calvi. You just don't like me, that's all. I seriously think you should take a long long holiday, Superintendent. Your obsession with me is beginning to cloud your judgement.'

Philip kept an edge of nastiness in his voice. They'd both of them played this scene before, and they both knew what it was about. The Superintendent gave an almost-smile, the slightest of gestures of recognition.

'Oh no, Mr Fletcher, clouding the issue is your speciality, isn't it? You've led us all round the houses, you have. When did you last see Shustikov?'

'Oh for heaven's sake!'

Philip broke away, took a few steps into the corner. The face-to-face confrontation was too wearing. He refixed the policeman with a frigid stare from a distance. The eyes that met him were a pair of ice-cubes.

'Aren't you a little senior to be running a missing persons inquiry, Superintendent? No wonder the police are always complaining about being overstretched! Don't you have any criminals to catch?'

'When did you last see Shustikov?'

'I've already told you. Ask Constable Wheeler.'

'I'm asking you.'

'And I'm not telling you.'

'Obstructing the police is a serious offence.'

'Whereas obstructing the public is fair game, is it? I've no idea where Shustikov is and I couldn't care less either.'

'I'd start caring very much if I was you, Mr Fletcher. An allegation has been made—'

'Balls.'

'Miss Pine—'

'Miss Pine is an hysterical raving besotted drunk. Sergei was drunk too but he didn't want to speak to her last night. Much · the same way as I feel about you, Superintendent. You think she's right? You really think Sergei popped his clogs and I had something to do with it? Arrest me, then. And when he turns up I'll sue you for every penny in the Police Federation's piggy bank. That'd make quite a story, wouldn't it? Make all the front pages, I'll bet: "Bungling Cop Cocks Up Again!" They'll probably drop you straight back down to inspector, you might even make the *Guinness Book of Records* for the shortest promotion in history. Come on, get your handcuffs out. Either that or piss off out of here. I'm getting fed up with this.'

There was a long pause. Philip concentrated on making his eyes expressionless, on trying not to blink. The policeman was a natural, not a flicker crossed his face. Philip held his ground.

'I simply wanted to ask a few questions, that's all,' said the Superintendent quietly, in an almost conciliatory tone.

· 'Then take me down to the station and we'll have a properly tape-recorded interview with my solicitor present, or wouldn't that be your style? What was it you said about the language of the playground? I think I still recognize the school bully when I see him. I do see your problem, though – with a witness like Melissa it's about the only tactic you've got; hers isn't the kind of testimony that's going to stand up under cross-examination, is it now? Or don't you agree? Well, if you don't, let's have it on the record. Arrest me!'

'Have you committed an offence, Mr Fletcher?'

'Does it matter? It clearly takes more than a complete absence of evidence to deter a man like you.'

'Evidence of what?'

'Whatever it is you think I've done.'

'And what have you done?'

'Wouldn't you like to know . . .'

The policeman sighed. He even essayed a light smile, though not with much success. He adopted a coaxing, half-rueful tone, but that wasn't quite right either: 'You're making this unnecessarily difficult, my friend . . .'

Philip winced. The heavy-handedness of his change of tack was almost laughably clumsy.

'Really, Superintendent,' he murmured reprovingly.

'All you have to do to clear up this unfortunate misunderstanding is produce Mr Shustikov.'

'Like a rabbit from a hat? You've got the wrong man. Try arresting Paul Daniels.'

'If nothing's the matter with Mr Shustikov, as you say, why should I have to arrest anyone?'

'Why indeed? Surely if one barking mad inebriated hysterical witness, namely Miss Pine, makes idiotic allegations refuted by two respectable and distinguished law-abiding citizens, it behoves the former to prove the allegation rather than the latter to refute it?'

'Two citizens?'

'Myself and Miss Fielding.'

'Ah yes. Miss Fielding. She, I take it, doesn't know where Mr Shustikov is either?'

'Why don't you ask her?'

'I might just do that.'

'She's probably in her dressing room. It's off the Studio Theatre, you have to go through the foyer.'

'Thanks for the directions.'

'As I said, Superintendent, I always try to be of assistance.'

'Very public-spirited, Mr Fletcher.'

'Try to sound as if you mean it, Superintendent Higginbottom.'

The policeman walked slowly to the door. He reached for the handle, but didn't turn it. He waited a moment, then turned back to face Philip. His eyes were even emptier and colder than before, and his voice even more expressionless.

'You develop a nose in this business,' he said. 'After twenty years you get to have a pretty good sense of smell. I think of myself as like a water diviner, holding his stick. Why do my nostrils twitch so violently whenever I'm around you?'

Philip shrugged. 'I'll have to change my aftershave.'

'You think you're very clever, don't you?'

'I shall be writing a letter of complaint to your superior officer, Superintendent Higginbottom,' said Philip with crisp hostility. 'Your behaviour is rude and boorish and falls considerably short of the standards expected in a senior officer. I shall say as much in my letter—'

'You're clever but you're full of shit.'

'I don't think I have anything more to say to you, Superintendent. Please leave.'

A slow, mirthless smile pushed up the corners of the policeman's mouth. He opened the door and started to walk out.

'I'll be back,' he said without looking over his shoulder. He closed the door firmly after him.

Philip fell against the wall. His head was spinning and his legs could barely support his weight. He slid slowly to the floor, like ice cream melting on a stick.

'The bastard!' He muttered weakly to himself. 'Bloody hell!'

He felt terrible. His nerves were shot and his head ached to buggery. Shakily he lit another cigarette, but it made his dry mouth burn. There was some mineral water on the dressing-room table. He pulled himself across the floor and gulped it from the bottle. He was feeling too uncoordinated to risk pouring it into a glass.

'How all occasions do inform against me . . .' he moaned to himself in the mirror.

He was aghast at his own reflection. The lack of sleep was evident in his red bagged eyes; the rest of his white drawn features a testament to his state of nervous near-collapse. No wonder Higginbottom had scented blood.

'Oh God, God! How weary, stale, flat and unprofitable . . . what am I going to do? How long will a man lie in the boot of a Ford Cortina ere he rots? How long before Higginbottom's twig of a nose starts to twitch around it? And how many years behind bars am I looking at?'

A lot, he decided. There was no chance he was going to get

away with being an accessory. If Shitski's body were discovered, Superintendent Higginbottom would see to it personally that he took the full rap.

'It's not fair!' Philip whimpered, pleading with himself in the mirror. 'I didn't even kill Richie Calvi! Why's everyone after me for crimes I haven't committed? How did I get into this ridiculous mess?'

He banged his forehead into his fists. It did nothing for his mounting headache, but the pain focused his anger: 'Bloody Dick Jones. It's your sodding fault . . .'

He clenched his fists even tighter. His knuckles were as white as his face.

'If I go down,' he muttered into the mirror, 'I'll bloody take Dick Jones with me.'

'Don't be stupid!' his reflection muttered back. 'Get a grip on yourself. You're not going down.'

'Oh yeah? Got any bright ideas then?'

'You've been in tighter situations than this.'

'None that I can recall.'

'They haven't got anything on you.'

'Yet.'

'It's just Melissa's word against yours.'

'Until they find the body.'

'They're not going to.'

'Supposing they don't – Melissa's not going to go away, you know.'

'Discredit her.'

'How?'

'You're halfway there already. If Higginbottom was sure she was telling the truth he'd have you banged up with or without a corpse. Prove she's lying.'

'She isn't.'

'I know that. You know that. Make sure no one else does.'

'Perhaps I should just let Natasha murder her too.'

'You could murder Higginbottom while you're at it.'

'And Jones.'

'Especially Jones.'

'If I'm going down might as well take the lot with me.'

'You're not going down . . .'

He held his own eyes in the mirror, stared himself out. His resolve had hardened, he felt calmer. He felt in control again. He didn't even jump in response to a sudden frantic hammering on the door.

'Come in—'

But Natasha didn't wait for his invitation. She threw herself into the room and into his arms in one fluent motion.

'Philip, I'm scared . . .'

He stroked her hair and murmured gently in her ear. He had only just mastered his own terror.

'Yes,' he said, soothing her, 'he can be quite a handful, can't he?'

'What?' She disengaged herself sharply. 'What are you talking about?'

'Superintendent Higginbottom.'

'You mean you knew he was coming to see me?'

'Well, I told him to.'

'Bastard!'

'Yes, he's not pleasant—'

'I mean you! Why didn't you warn me he was coming?'

'That was hardly possible.'

'Why did you tell him to see me?'

'To back up my story, of course. Besides, I needed to get him off my back.'

'And on to mine! You selfish bastard!'

'Really, Natasha, he was going to see you anyway. I think—'

'Oh, I wish you would!' She stamped her foot. She was quivering all over. 'Never fear, you said, you'd think of a way out of this. Well?'

'Well what?'

'Well what have you thought? You can't leave him in the boot much longer, you know, he'll start to smell.'

'I know.'

'Then what do you intend to do about it?'

'Keep your voice down. Shouting won't help.'

'God, you're infuriating sometimes!'

'You're not all sweetness and light yourself. What did you tell Higginbottom?'

'The usual. He's a nasty piece of work, gave me the creeps. Brr! I got the feeling he didn't believe a word I was saying ... I'm sorry I shouted.'

'That's all right. I'm not at my best myself.'

'Can I have a hug?'

She fell into his arms again, only this time she didn't hang on him like a rag doll: her hands clawed and kneaded him passionately; he considered it only polite to respond in kind.

'I'm sorry about those reviews,' she said huskily, nuzzling his ear. 'They're fools, they know nothing. Let me make it up to you ...'

She undid his belt and top button and slid a hand into his waistband.

'You do get turned on at the oddest times,' he told her.

'I'm not alone,' she answered.

As she had the evidence in hand Philip felt it would have been disingenuous to deny it. Instead he began unzipping her skirt.

There was a loud knock on the door.

'Philip?' a voice called from outside.

'Er, hang on ...'

They sprang apart like schoolkids caught snogging in the bicycle sheds. After a few stretched moments of drastic re-buttoning, Philip yanked open the door. It was the stage manager.

'Sorry to bother you, it's Natasha I'm after really ...' He waved a piece of paper at her. 'Well, Sergei actually, but I wonder if you could give him this message. Front of House took it, it's from the arts centre in Bristol, some bloke called Alan. They want him to call them about Friday. I put the number on the bottom.'

'Thanks ...' said Natasha distractedly, taking the paper.

Philip cleared his throat.

'We were just going over some lines,' he explained.

'Oh, right ... you can use the stage if you like.'

The stage manager's bored tone suggested that he couldn't have cared less. Philip thanked him anyway. When he had gone, he locked the door.

'Better late than never, I suppose,' Natasha murmured.

Philip felt himself come out in a cold sweat again. What if it had been Higginbottom? What if he had just come in without waiting to be asked and found the two of them locked in their embrace?

'We've got to be careful,' Philip muttered crossly, lighting a cigarette.

'Can I have one?' asked Natasha.

'I thought you didn't?'

'I didn't.'

He did his Paul Henreid act and lit two cigarettes. She stroked his hand with a finger as she took hers. The bit of paper the stage manager had given her was scrunched up in her palm.

'Yuck! How disgusting!' she said, breaking into a fit of coughing after her first drag. She went straight to the ashtray and jabbed out her cigarette. 'Revolting habit, I don't—'

'Quiet!' said Philip suddenly.

'What is it?'

'I'm thinking . . .'

He went over and took the paper from her. He smoothed it out and read the message.

'I told you about it,' she explained. 'In the pub, yesterday. Sergei's meant – was meant – to open the Stanislavsky Centre on Friday. I can't remember all the details.'

'Have you got them?'

'Yes. They're in the flat. Alan wrote Sergei a letter.'

'Who?'

'The chap who runs it, he's called Alan Fermon. Used to be an actor, I worked with him about ten years ago.'

'Does he know Sergei?'

'No, no, never met him. He wrote to me when we came back from America, asked me to ask Sergei. I said I would, but frankly I was surprised when Sergei agreed to it. He usually hated doing anything like that.'

'He was probably flattered at being mentioned in the same breath as Stanislavsky.'

'Maybe, Alan certainly laid it on thick. Philip, what on earth are you thinking?'

He folded the piece of paper carefully and put it away in his wallet. He sat himself on the edge of the dressing-room table and smoked and thought hard. She could see him concentrating and she let him be. After half a minute or so he looked up and smiled at her slyly.

'It's a long time since we were both in Bristol, isn't it? I think maybe we should pay our old haunts a visit . . .'

# 15

Act II was just beginning. Enter Pompey, stage right:

If the great gods be just, they shall assist
The deeds of justest men.

'Fat chance!' muttered Seymour Loseby in the wings. Menecrates burbled on:

Know, worthy Pompey,
That what they do delay, they not deny.

'Pompous arsehole,' observed Seymour. 'Come on, dear, get on with it. We've two more hours of this rubbish to get through and I need a drink already.'

'Anyone would think you'd been doing it for six months,' said Philip, who was also waiting for his cue.

'What a hideous thought!' responded Seymour, pulling a face. 'Was it really only yesterday we opened? My mind's a blank.'

'Your mind's been a blank for as long as I've known you, Seymour.'

'You savoury tart!'

'Ssh, please!' said the stage manager, swivelling round in his chair and tapping his lips with a finger. Seymour lowered his voice marginally:

'Where'd you get to last night, by the way? We all convened at my place, had a rather jolly little party. Your absence was noted.'

'I'm afraid I drew the short straw. I ended up minding Shitski.'

'Please don't mention that name again! I left the garlic in my dressing room.'

'Either you're deluding yourself or your deodorant's gone off.'

'A hit, a palpable hit! Was Natasha with you?'

'No, she and Shitski weren't really seeing eye to eye last night, as you might imagine. He crashed out at my place.'

'How distressing for you. Where's the old bastard tonight?'

'Out front.'

'Is he? Why hasn't he given us any notes?'

'I think he's still sulking.'

'Well, I won't complain. The last twenty-four hours have been blissfully quiet. I suppose he'll come throwing his weight around backstage and ruin all that after the show.'

'Oh, I don't think so. Apparently they're shooting off to Bristol straight afterwards.'

'Bristol?'

'He's got some do there tomorrow. Natasha's driving him.'

'They're on speaking terms again?'

'Fingers crossed.'

'I don't think I will cross mine, thank you very much. The sooner she's shot of him, the better. As I was telling her—'

'Ssh! Quiet please!' hissed the stage manager.

Seymour clapped a hand over his mouth and made a wide-eyed guilty mime. It was a gesture Philip found largely unconvincing.

'Bristol?' repeated Superintendent Higginbottom incredulously.

'That's right, sir,' affirmed Constable Wheeler. 'He's off there tonight.'

The superintendent swore softly. Softly, but far from mildly.

'Really, sir,' Constable Wheeler insisted. 'I took the call myself. About an hour and a half ago.'

'When?'

'An hour and a half. About—'

'Yes, I can work it out. Why the hell didn't you call me earlier?'

'I'm sorry, sir, I didn't know where to get hold of you.'

The superintendent lowered the receiver and scowled about him menacingly. The hospital corridor was crowded and noisy, the Perspex bubble over the payphone a useless gesture towards soundproofing. A tannoy someone had forgotten to switch off was hissing on the wall above. He pressed the phone back hard against one ear, and covered the other ear with his palm.

'You spoke to him personally, did you?'

'Yes, sir, he asked to speak to me.'

'What did he sound like?'

'Well, er . . . a bit foreign—'

'But did he sound all right?'

'Oh . . . well, I think he'd been drinking, but—'

'How did you know it was him?'

'Sorry, sir?'

'The man you spoke to – he said he was Shustikov, right?'

'Yes, that's—'

'Have you spoken to him before?'

'Well, no—'

'Have you ever met him?'

'No.'

'Then how did you know it was him?'

'Well, he said he was . . . him.'

'And where was he?'

'I'm not sure—'

'Didn't you ask?'

'Yes I did, but he didn't tell me.'

'Why not?'

'I don't know, sir.'

'Why wouldn't he answer the question? What's he hiding?'

'I don't know, sir. He said he couldn't hear me very well, he was in a call box, like yourself.'

'But he said he was going to Bristol tonight?'

'That's right, sir. I think he was going to see some Russian bloke, Stan something, I wrote it down.'

'All right, Constable, this is what I want you to do. Get round to his place, that flat in Hampstead he shares with his bird, and see if he's there. If he isn't, stake it out, and call me the moment anyone turns up. Wait there till I call you.'

'How long—'

'Look, don't ask questions, Constable, just get your arse over there bloody fast. OK?'

Superintendent Higginbottom rammed down the phone. He turned and marched aggressively across the shiny clackety floor towards the lifts in the corner.

The interval had just begun.

'Philip, could you give me a hand?' Natasha asked as she swept by him in the corridor.

'Sorry, Seymour,' said Philip, excusing himself to his friend and breaking off their conversation. He followed her into her dressing room and closed the door.

'Could you unzip me, please?' she asked.

'Nothing could give me greater pleasure.'

'Nothing? Really, Mr Fletcher, what a sheltered life you must lead . . .'

He leant against the door and silently admired her body as she changed her costume.

'Enjoying the show?' she enquired.

'Mm. Thank you.'

'What were you telling Seymour?'

'Everything we want him to know. Everyone else in the company will know it inside ten minutes. That's the beauty of Seymour.'

'I told Sally about Bristol too. She's quite a chatterbox.'

'Good. Between them and Constable Wheeler we should have it pretty well covered.'

'Did he really think you were Sergei?'

'Why shouldn't he?'

'I don't know . . . the other one wouldn't have believed you.'

'You mean Higginbottom? I rang the station first to check that he wasn't around. Then I rang back and asked for the constable.'

'And he didn't suspect anything?'

143

'Natasha, relax. Wheeler doesn't know what Sergei sounds like. As far as he's concerned Sergei sounds like me. My Russian accent's pretty good, you know. You can hear for yourself later.'

'I hope to God you're right about this, Philip. Did you call Alan Fermon?'

'He wasn't in. I wish I knew a little more of what he wanted.'

'I'm sorry I couldn't find the letter, Sergei must have thrown it away. Philip, this is very risky.'

'Of course it is, but it's our only chance. What's that line in act two? "Who seeks, and will not take when once 'tis offer'd/Shall never find it more." It's the only chance we've got; it's the only game in town. Shall I zip you up?'

'If you have to.'

'Needs must . . . knock 'em dead.'

He brushed his lips against her forehead, taking care not to smudge her make-up. She returned his smile knowingly.

'You should be careful who you say that to.'

Melissa Pine was sitting up in her hospital bed when Superintendent Higginbottom burst into her room.

'Please!' she said crossly, pulling up the covers in a futile display of modesty. 'Don't you ever knock?'

'He's going to Bristol,' said the policeman firmly, ignoring her protest.

'Who?'

'Who'd you think? The Wizard of Oz? Sergei bloody Shustikov, that's who.'

Melissa burrowed a little deeper under the covers.

'Please don't shout!' she exclaimed weakly. 'I'm ill.'

The policeman snatched a chair and threw himself down beside her.

'You'll be a lot worse than ill, miss, if I find you've been pissing me about. Shustikov rang in to the station an hour and a half ago. He spoke to the lad on duty.'

Melissa's drawn pale face became still whiter. 'That's impossible.'

'You don't say? You still think he's dead, do you?'

'Yes! Yes, yes, yes! I saw it with my own eyes! They killed him.'

'Then who was it rang the station? Doris Stokes?'

Melissa sat up angrily. The colour was back in her cheeks. 'It was an impostor!'

The superintendent sat still and stared her out. When she didn't flinch he got up slowly and walked to the window. He looked at his watch.

'Let's just suppose you're right . . .' he began.

'There's nothing to suppose!' she snapped at him.

She sounded impressively sure of herself, but then that was how she had come across all along. She meant what she was saying, he had no doubt about that. By her own admission she'd been drunk the night before, and ordinarily he'd have thrown a compromised testimony like hers out without a second thought, but there was a complicating factor. The Philip Fletcher factor. It was sheer chance that had involved him in this business. He had just happened to be passing the desk first thing that morning and had heard the duty sergeant read Fletcher's name aloud from Wheeler's report. Sheer chance – or something more? Had it been fate?

'How are you feeling?' he asked her, with what he no doubt took for kindness.

'I'm not doolally, if that's what you mean!' Melissa answered angrily, having failed to spot the attempted pleasantness.

'I'm not saying you are,' he answered in his more usual tone. 'I mean, are you fit enough to discharge yourself?'

'I might be . . . Why?'

He came back and stood over the bed. His face was as hard and calculating as his voice: 'Because if there is an impostor going about the place I can't think of anyone better to unmask him. Can you?'

The audience was applauding enthusiastically.

'I think we'll do one more,' Philip muttered through his fixed grinning teeth as he bowed low.

'Okay,' Natasha muttered back on his right.

'Only one?' chipped in Seymour.

145

'Don't want to milk it, dear,' Philip answered, as he lifted his head triumphantly to the gods. It being the Riverside Studios there were no gods, but it was hard to forgo the habit of a lifetime.

Having disposed of the final bow the cast peeled off to left and right, Natasha leading one half, Philip the other.

'Coming for a drink?' enquired Seymour, as they reached the safe berth of the wings.

'Not tonight,' replied Philip. 'I've a bit of a headache, I need an early night.'

'My dear old thing, whatever happened to your staying power? Anyone would think you were my age!'

'No one's your age, Seymour.'

'I find your cruelty oddly exciting, Philip.'

'I know. Please excuse me, I'm going to shoot off quickly. I want to avoid Shitski.'

'Yuck! I'd forgotten about him.'

'Must dash. See you tomorrow.'

Philip hurried to his dressing room and changed quickly. He didn't bother to remove his make-up. On his way out front he passed Sally in the corridor.

'You haven't seen Shitski about, have you?' he whispered anxiously, pulling up his collar in a furtive gesture.

'Er, no. Is he around?'

Philip nodded vigorously.

'And in a filthy temper too. I'd stay clear of him if I was you.'

'I will!' she answered back, sounding as if she meant it. 'I suppose he's here to meet Natasha. They're going off to Bristol, you know.'

'Oh yes, so they are. Good night. Beware the foul fiend!'

He scurried on out. He had been so quick that many of the audience were still milling about in the foyer. He was recognized, of course, and he heard the gratifying whisper of his name trailing in his wake, but he was not molested. The minicab he had ordered earlier was waiting outside.

He timed the journey home at twenty-seven minutes. It was

a quarter to midnight when he mounted the stairs to his flat, much too late to be making any social calls. Nonetheless he went on up to the third floor and rang the bell of the flat above his own.

'I'm so terribly sorry to trouble you at this hour,' he said to the young man in dressing gown and pyjamas who answered the door, 'but I must have picked up some of your mail this morning by mistake. Did I wake you?'

'Oh, no,' the man answered with a smile, taking the two letters which Philip had filched from the communal hall earlier. His neighbour did something in the City and had always left in the morning before the post. 'Thanks very much. I was just reading, actually.'

'Oh?'

The man seemed to want to chat. Philip didn't, but having disturbed him so late he felt obliged to go through the motions. Normally he avoided his neighbours, he hadn't even known the man's name before examining the letters. It was Malcolm.

'All right then, Malcolm,' said Philip cheerfully, when he had endured three minutes or so of his neighbour's banal enquiries about the show, his past television roles and his future prospects (Malcolm's interest in his career considerably exceeded his own interest in Malcolm's). 'I'm afraid I'm feeling whacked! I'd better turn in.'

'Ah, right. I'll see you around then.'

Philip hoped not.

He went downstairs to his own flat. His spare set of make-up was lying on the bathroom chair. Next to it was a grey wig on a block and a set of matching whiskers, which he had selected earlier from his extensive collection. He stripped to the waist and removed his stage make-up. Just as he was finishing, his door buzzer sounded.

It was the outside door. Who could possibly be visiting at this hour? It didn't take him long to figure it out. He went into the bedroom and changed quickly into his pyjamas. The buzzer sounded again.

'Yes, who is it?' he demanded grumpily into the intercom.

'It's Constable Wheeler, sir,' came the rather hesitant reply. 'Sorry to bother you at this hour, I was wondering—'

'You'd better come on up,' said Philip brusquely. He pressed the door release.

'Do you know what time it is?' he demanded crossly, as Constable Wheeler plonked his size-eleven feet down across the threshold. The young policeman turned bright red.

'I'm really terribly sorry to bother you, sir,' he stammered uneasily. 'I'm, er, looking for Mr Shistikov.'

Philip gave him his blankest stare.

'Sergei?' he said incredulously. 'Sergei's gone to Bristol.'

'Oh he has, has he? Ah right, yes he did say he was going there.'

'So what on earth are you doing looking for him here, Constable?'

The policeman made an incoherent, strangled sort of noise. Philip regarded him coldly.

'I beg your pardon?'

'Just following orders, sir. Er, you wouldn't happen to know where exactly he's staying in Bristol, would you, sir?'

'No, I would not.'

'Ah, right . . . well, sorry to bother you, sir.'

'I should think so.'

'Right, well, I'll be off then. Good n—'

'Good night, Constable!' said Philip crisply, and slammed the door in his face.

He turned the light back off and crept over to the window. Through a crack in the curtains he witnessed the policeman climb into his car and speak briefly into his radio, before starting his engine and driving off. Philip permitted himself a smug smile before returning to the bathroom.

His make-up took him twenty minutes. There wasn't much to it besides the whiskers and wig, just a grey thickening of the eyebrows and a vinous stipple to the cheeks, a bagatelle to a skilled master of concealment such as he. It was appropriate that he should be returning to Bristol in disguise, for it was there that he had laid the foundations of his reputation

148

as a character actor. When he was ready he put on his overcoat and collected his overnight bag, prepacked with essentials, from the bedroom. He checked that the street outside was empty, then slipped out quietly and crossed Highbury Fields at the trot.

He started to walk along Upper Street and picked up a taxi almost immediately. He asked to be taken to Hammersmith Broadway. The return journey lasted twenty-six minutes.

He took his time walking down to the theatre. After smoking a leisurely cigarette he reconnoitred around River Terrace. There was no one about. At one o'clock precisely he tapped lightly on the Studio exit. Natasha opened it from within and he stepped inside.

Briefly they embraced. She felt tense, but sounded calm.

'You were right,' she told him. 'Higginbottom came here.'

'He didn't see you?'

'No.'

He took a torch from his overnight bag and switched it on. They began to make their way to the stage.

'Where did you hide?' he asked.

'In Wardrobe. I got into a skip, like you suggested, made myself comfortable and closed the lid.'

'You're sure no one saw you?'

'Positive. I made sure Sally and Seymour clocked me leaving, then I doubled back on myself, went round the other side of the stage. The stage manager and the ASMs were on the set, but they didn't see me. I heard them talking about Higginbottom later. He had Melissa with him.'

'Did he now? Good thing he didn't get here any earlier. That was lucky.'

He told her about Constable Wheeler's visit. 'Higginbottom must have sent him. I don't know why but he doesn't seem to trust me. Well, that's two people saw me at my flat tonight. Let him suspect me now!'

'Philip, what is it between you and him?'

'It's a personal vendetta, I'm afraid. Here we are . . .'

They stopped by the derelict Ford Cortina in the middle

of the stage. It was all but submerged in polystyrene snow flakes. They began scooping them away.

'Did you get the tools?' he asked.

'They're in the car.'

The garden flat she and Sergei had been renting came with a fully equipped shed. She had promised to bring a spade.

'And the trolley?'

'Over there.'

It was in the wings, complete with the bungee straps he had left hanging from it yesterday. While she went and got it he balanced the torch in the convenient vee of the nearest piece of scaffolding and pointed the beam at the car. Then he opened the boot.

There was a faint mildewy smell inside, though whether it was of decomposing metal or flesh he couldn't have said; he was only used to dealing with fresh corpses. The flesh was cold and waxy to the touch. The knees were bent foetally up into the stomach.

'Give me a hand, will you?'

He took hold of the body under the arms, she managed the feet. There was no hesitation from her, no hint of the gingerliness he himself felt and repressed. Neither of them looked at the face.

'On the count of three . . .'

They heaved. His face was screwed up hard like a weight-lifter's, his teeth gritted against the pain. His eyes were closed, too, though more in dread than agony. This moment he had feared above the rest; this was the scene where the arc lights stuttered accusingly to life, and Higginbottom leapt with handcuffs and a mocking sneer from behind the arras . . .

Nothing happened. Between them they shifted the lumpen dead-weight out of the boot and laid it down on the trolley. They took a moment leaning against each other for support, and got back their breath. He was getting too old for this lark.

'Empty his pockets,' he said.

He didn't need to tell her; they had planned it thoroughly. They spoke to each other for reassurance, to comfort themselves in their grisly work. While she dredged for his possessions he examined the clothes for labels. There was a laundry tab in the trouser waistband and a tailor's patch on the jacket lining. He cut them both out with a pair of sharp scissors, and put them with the cigarettes, the wallet, the keys that she had retrieved into a plastic bag. He would have liked to strip the body altogether, but its condition after thirty hours made that impractical.

'Have you decided what we're going to do with him?' she asked as she trawled his pockets.

'I'm afraid we will have to bury him; I just can't think of anything better. By the way, where's his passport?'

'His passport? It's in a drawer at home, I think.'

'Is it Russian?'

'Oh no, he was given asylum. It's British. What are you thinking of?'

'I'll tell you later. Most important thing for now is to find somewhere to bury him.'

It would have to be somewhere on the way back from Bristol. While others stopped to picnic or relieve themselves, they would be gravedigging, out in some godforsaken spot he didn't know yet but could only hope existed. He hated the vagueness of it all, but what else could they do? They had to dispose of the body somehow, and do it soon. He knew how flawed the plan was – had he not warned her of promiscuous sniffing country dogs, dismissed out of hand the very plan he now proposed? But circumstances had changed. Risks had to be run. And if some sharp-nosed hound should dig him up, they could at least do all in their power to muffle his identity.

'You're sure about dental records?' he asked.

'Positive. He never had treatment over here. He had toothache last year in Ottawa and I think he saw someone then, but the only records will be back in Russia.'

And who would think of checking there? The longer the body lay in the ground, the better their chances. Decay and anonymity made bedfellows six feet under. To what base uses may we be returned?

Imperious Caesar, dead, and turn'd to clay,
Might stop a hole to keep the wind away.

If only.

They bound the body to the trolley with straps and the camel blanket, Sergei's shroud. Then Philip wheeled him into the wings while Natasha covered their tracks with polystyrene shavings. They crossed together to the Studio Theatre, she opening doors and guiding him with the torch. He waited by the exit at the top of the ramp while she scouted ahead for ambushing hysterics. None was spotted. The little backstreet was as dark and quiet as it had been yesterday.

'Which car?' he whispered.

It was a blue saloon. She had hired it in the afternoon, at his insistence. She hadn't seen the point.

'The police could check the licence number of your car,' he had explained patiently. 'It may be the slimmest of risks, but do you really want to be pulled over with Sergei in the back? Get something with a big boot.'

She had. Putting Sergei in was easier than pulling him out of the last one: they stood the trolley up next to the bumper, untied the body and more or less rolled it in. Natasha waited in the car while Philip took the trolley back to the theatre. She had the engine idling on his return.

They drove out of Crisp Road, past the old Hammersmith Odeon and on to the Broadway. It was gone half past one and there was little traffic. It took only a few minutes to reach the motorway.

'Don't drive too fast,' he warned her. 'We don't want to be stopped for speeding.'

'We've a long way to go,' she said, but she took her foot a little off the pedal. They cruised down the M4 at something over 80 m.p.h.

They pulled off at junction 18 a little after 3 a.m. Philip had been dozing. He woke as she pulled into the forecourt of the motel.

'I'll go and sign in,' she said.

'Shall I come?'

'No need.'

It was true, but he hoped that she wasn't reluctant to be seen with him. She would have no choice tomorrow. He checked his whiskers and wig in the mirror, just in case someone should glance in. His precautions were perhaps over-elaborate, but it was a form of compensation for the morrow, when nothing could be elaborate enough: from now on they would be so far out on a limb that a tremor might send them crashing to the ground as easily as an earthquake.

'We're over there,' said Natasha on her return, indicating the end of a row of chalet-like buildings. 'I'll repark the car.'

She drove them over. He took out their bags and waited for her to lock up.

'Let's hope no one steals it,' he murmured.

'Don't . . .'

She unlocked the door to their chalet and they went in. It was an American-type motel in an English rural style, self-contained units with fake gables and Tudor beams generously spaced around the grounds of what had once been a little country inn. Natasha had booked it.

'Well chosen,' he commented, drawing the curtains. There were no lights on in the neighbouring chalets and the car park had seemed three-quarters empty. At the same time they were only forty minutes away from Bristol city centre.

'I used to come here with Julian,' she said, opening her case and taking out a washbag. 'Shall I use the bathroom first?'

He nodded. He kicked off his shoes and sat back on the bed. He heard the shower being switched on next door.

'Lucky Julian,' he muttered to himself.

He felt an acute stab of jealousy as he imagined the two of them driving into the forecourt in Julian Carne's red MG. When had they been here? At weekends, perhaps, when Julian was just visiting after the run of *The White Devil* had ended. Perhaps they'd used this very room, this very rank enseamèd bed, to snatch sex by the hour while somewhere else Philip had been pining away his miserable inadequate life. Unpleasant images queued up for attention in his memory. He savoured them with bitter relish.

'Stop it!' he told himself crossly. The combination of jealousy and self-pity was a sickening brew. He felt nauseous.

'Stop what?' asked Natasha innocently, coming out of the bathroom, still drying herself with a towel.

'Nothing,' he answered brusquely, getting up and going past her.

He snatched up his bag as he went into the bathroom. He locked the door, which was hardly necessary, and took out his make-up and wig block. He removed his false hair carefully (the pieces were superbly made and required only a dab of spirit gum) and brushed it out. A handful of cream cleansed his face.

'What are you doing here?' he asked himself in the mirror. 'What do you want? What does she want?'

He couldn't work her out. She was so composed, so controlled. If it was only an act she might crack up again at any moment, a terrifying thought, but so far the performance had been seamless. How was she managing it? His own face (he could see it now) was etched with strain; hers wasn't. And why had she just dropped Julian into the conversation, oh so casually? What was she playing at? How had she acquired her appalling taste in men?

'Where does that leave me?' he wondered.

He stripped and got into the shower. It revived him a little. It was late and he'd hardly slept the previous night. He was exhausted. It must have been his tiredness that was making him so irritable. He wondered if Julian had stood under this same shower head, washing away the smell of Natasha.

He made the shower hotter. Steam rose, the scalding pins of water made him yelp. He turned the tap off suddenly and jumped out.

There was a little hotel hand-towel on the rail. He hadn't packed one himself. He unlocked the door and opened it an inch.

'Could I borrow your towel, please?'

She appeared in front of the door. She pushed it open, making him step back. She was wearing an amused and slightly ironical look, and her towel.

'You mean this?' she said.

She lifted the end where it was tucked in above her cleavage and gently shook it loose. The towel fell away.

'Why, Mr Fletcher, you're all naked . . .'

That made two of them. They stood for a moment appreciating each other. He didn't feel quite so tired any more.

'Let's go next door,' he said, in a dry voice.

'Let's,' she answered softly, taking him by the hand and leading him over to the bed. They fell down on it together.

Sleep? he thought. Who needs it?

# *16*

Philip had last been in Bristol seven years previously, a brief two-day visit to record a radio play. The city centre had changed, as all city centres change, but as they drove up the hill of Park Street and into Whiteladies Road, familiar sights queued up to reassure him. On the left he saw a familiar pub and a curry house where many a post-performance appetite had been assuaged; on the right the BBC building, of which his keenest memory was sharing a corridor with a member of the natural history unit and an incontinent baby elephant. In his time he had suffered keenly for his art.

'I think this is right,' Natasha murmured uncertainly, turning off the main road just before they hit the Downs.

They drove into a seemingly deserted and somewhat desolate side street. A builder's van all but blocked off access and Natasha bashed her wing mirror squeezing past. In front of them was a long low Victorian building that might once have been a school. One half was obscured by scaffolding and the forecourt was covered in piles of brick and sand.

'Looks just like the set,' Philip observed.

'I'll go and check it out,' said Natasha. 'You'd better wait here.'

Why should he have waited? he wondered, as he watched her thread her way through the heaps of building material on her way round to the side of the building. Was she still loath to be seen with him?

'Too late now . . .' he said to himself, turning the driving mirror towards his face and giving his appearance a last redundant check. He looked pretty good. His make-up had been much more thorough today than yesterday, even incorporating a false plastic nose, the nostrils fleshed out with putty to suggest a faintly Asiatic look. Natasha had wondered why he was taking such pains, but to a perfectionist like him they were not pains at all. He touched the grey wig and the whiskers, making sure they were secure. There wasn't a hair out of place.

Someone out in the yard wolf-whistled. Philip watched in amusement as Natasha, a picture of self-conscious disdain, swanned into the building. He sympathized with the whistler. She looked terrific. And she had looked even better last night as she was giving him her whirlwind tutorial in sins of the flesh, advanced level. It had been a night of such relentless smouldering debauchery that he was surprised the bedclothes hadn't ignited. It might even have been worth waiting fifteen years for an experience like that. At least he'd always have last night to remember, even if it did all go horribly wrong and he spent the next fifteen years in maximum security.

Sweat ran down his temples. He wasn't feeling at his best. Outwardly he may have seemed calm, but inside he was a mess of nerves. He was tired too – hardly surprising after last night. It was stuffy in the car. He got out. Where had Natasha got to? It was past eleven thirty, the time they were meant to arrive, and it looked suspiciously like the wrong address. He supposed that he had better stay put, in case she came back and they missed each other. He lit a cigarette and sucked on it hungrily. After a long restless pause he walked over to the entrance.

It had definitely once been a school – he could just make out two faded signs on either side of the main gates, one reading 'Girls', the other 'Boys'. Some tram-lines on the fore-court indicated a playing area, though they were scarcely visible underneath the piles of rubble. The half of the building free of scaffolding seemed much cleaner than the other side, but the amount of junk lying about indicated that more than renovation was at stake. The main work appeared to be going on around the corner, from whence there came a mechanical whirring noise. He went to have a look.

The wall at the end of the building had been partly demolished. Rope-lines extended out from the gap and enclosed a large rectangular area, pretty much all of the space left within the high brick wall that marked the perimeter of the old school. It looked like it was going to be an annexe, connected to the main building by a corridor, though at the moment there wasn't much more within the rope-lines than a hole in the ground. It was a big job, he wondered where on earth they'd got the money. Theatres and arts centres all over the country were threatened with closure, not even the Bristol Old Vic was safe. He supposed that somebody must have been keeping his tongue firmly glued to the right arse at the Arts Council. Questions of artistic merit, as ever, would have had sod all to do with it.

The mechanical noise came from a concrete mixer, which was tipped over the edge of the hole and was in the act of emptying its bowl of grey wet sludge over the foundations. The paltry load made little impression on the gaping maw in the earth.

'Put that out!' a voice hissed in his ear.

It was Natasha. She had appeared suddenly from out of the side of the half-demolished wall. She looked cross.

'You know he only smokes these!' she said hoarsely, advancing towards him and thrusting at him the half-empty packet of Gauloises she had retrieved from Sergei's pockets. 'Put it out!'

Reluctantly Philip tossed his cigarette into the concrete at the bottom of the hole. Natasha took his arm. He hoped she didn't notice that it was trembling.

'Apparently this is the back entrance,' she told him. 'Alan's waiting for us. You've got to give a talk.'

'A what?'

'Sergei agreed to talk about his work, apparently. I'm sorry, I didn't know anything about it, I'm sure it won't last – damn! Here's Alan!'

A small wan man with ungroomed hair and a droopy moustache appeared through the gap in the wall. Philip felt the pressure on his arm tighten.

'He hadn't gone far!' Natasha announced gaily, thrusting Philip forward. 'Alan, this is Sergei Shustikov.'

158

'Oh, right!' Alan Fermon extended a thin bony hand. 'I'm honoured to meet you.'

They shook hands. Alan indicated their surroundings with an amused shrug: 'What do you think of our little pad then?'

Philip put on an indifferent air. He concentrated on a low phlegmatic pitching of the voice. 'Your pad is shit heap.' he growled above the din of the cement mixer, using his best early-Bond multipurpose SMERSH voice.

Alan Fermon laughed uncertainly.

'Yeah, well, we've got a bit behind on the building, as you can see, but we're still hoping to have the new annexe complete in three months and then—'

'Yuargh!'

Philip flung his hand dismissively at the Arts supremo, who flinched.

'I no want to hear this shit! I am thirsty. Get me coffee. Now!'

Philip brushed past him in a sulk, kicking over a loose pile of bricks for good measure as he passed. He went through the hole in the wall, between the two rope-lines, and into the building.

'Er, stop!' Alan Fermon called out feebly behind him.

But Philip was suffering from the most massive adrenaline surge he had ever experienced. If the wall hadn't already been removed he might have gone through it notwithstanding, like a hyperactive Incredible Hulk. The build-up of tension within him had reached its critical mass, it exploded out of him like champagne from a racing driver's bottle. He hadn't overacted this badly since his first season as a juvenile in Windsor rep.

In front of him was a newly built brick wall, bare apart from an incongruous curtain of black material hanging down at one end and a shiny bright-red fire extinguisher on a bracket at the other. Between them stood an unpainted heavy swing-door. He threw it open and steamed on through.

He found himself on a small apron stage surrounded on three sides by a raised auditorium. About thirty people were in the central section of the audience. They were listening to a man who was seated on a kind of high barstool in the middle of the stage.

Philip stopped dead in front of the swing-door. Everyone was looking at him, including the man on the barstool he had so rudely interrupted. The man was very young, fair and freckled, and wore a big boyish grin, which he turned on Philip. Philip gaped back at him blankly.

It was Ben Ferris.

'Oh hi!' said the theatrical boy wonder, bouncing off his barstool and springing towards him with his right hand extended. 'You must be Sergei Shustikov.'

Philip stood rigidly, his arms pinned to his sides, ignoring the proffered hand.

'Who the shit you expect?' he croaked. 'Boris Yeltsin?'

Philip spun on his heels and crashed back out again through the swing-door. Alan and Natasha were waiting for him on the other side.

'Er, I was meant to introduce you, actually . . .' said Alan in a bewildered voice.

Natasha seized Philip by the arm.

'Sergei! What are you doing?'

Philip didn't have the slightest idea. Somewhere within the unfocused pulp of his brain he was trying to imagine how his role-model would have behaved in this situation. Badly, he concluded.

'Bah! Take your hand off me, you stupid woman!'

He flung Natasha away with a barely pulled forearm smash. He grabbed Alan Fermon by the lapels.

'What the shit goes on here?' he demanded furiously.

'So-so-sorry?' stammered Alan, his eyes widening with alarm.

'You shit will be, mister! I am here to open Stanislavsky Centre, no? What is meaning of this damn Ben Ferris shit?'

'I'm sorry, but – but you agreed to it!'

'I agree to it? When I agree to it?'

Philip turned angrily on Natasha.

'Why the shit you not tell me I agree to it, you stupid woman?'

'Because I didn't know!' Natasha shouted back at him. 'Don't you talk to me like that, you bastard!'

'You shit useless bitch!'

'Fuck you!'

For a moment Philip thought she was going to kick him, but she controlled herself.

'Sergei!' she snapped in a voice full of warning. 'For God's sake, get a grip!'

It was sound advice. With a snarl he released Alan's lapels. 'I ask for shit coffee? Where is it?'

'Um, I was just going to—'

Philip stamped his foot.

'I want it now!' he screamed furiously. 'Not shit yesterday, not shit three weeks ago, shit now!'

'Oh right . . . Hang on, I'm just going . . .'

Alan scurried off nervously through the swing-door. As it fell back into place after him Philip caught a brief glimpse of Ben Ferris and thirty other faces, all transfixed with astonishment.

'Philip!' Natasha hissed, grabbing him roughly by the arms. 'What are you playing at?'

'I thought I was here to open the sodding centre!' he spat back. 'What the hell's going on?'

'You are here to open the centre. Look!'

She lifted up the edge of the black curtain on the wall behind them. There was an inscribed brass plaque underneath, bearing the names Shustikov and Stanislavsky and the date.

'What's that out there then?' he demanded, waving his thumb in the direction of the stage.

'Philip, it's not my fault, I didn't know . . . Alan wrote Sergei a letter, I'm sorry, I didn't see it. Look, the unveiling's scheduled for twelve. You've just got to go out there for ten minutes or so, that's all, then we can scoot.'

'But what am I supposed to do? What's going on? What's Ben Ferris doing here?'

'That's Ben Ferris, is it?'

'Of course it's Ben bloody Ferris, unless Dick Jones has

murdered him too and we're all bloody impersonating each other!'

'Philip, keep your voice down! Don't take it out on me, I'm as much in the dark as you are. Take deep breaths!'

'What bloody good will that do? You're a fat lot of help!'

'Philip, you're supposed to behave as badly as Sergei. Not worse.'

'If taking deep breaths was the best advice you could offer him, then I sympathize with his irascibility. I need a cigarette.'

'Don't!'

She tried to snatch the packet from him, but he turned away, extracted, lit and dragged on a Rothmans before she could stop him.

'Put it out!' she demanded crossly, just as the swing-door behind them opened and Alan Fermon returned bearing a steaming plastic cup.

'Go to hell, shit stupid woman,' Philip grumbled, putting back on his thick bass.

'Sergei!' Natasha said through gritted teeth. 'You don't smoke those!'

'Bah!' Philip pulled from his pocket the packet of Gauloises she had given him and waved it under her nose. 'You want me smoke this shit? I no want smoke that shit! I want smoke this shit!'

He took a deep defiant drag of his cigarette.

'Um, would you like milk and sugar?' Alan asked hesitantly.

'Niet!' said Philip brusquely, snatching the plastic cup from him. 'I like it black.'

'No you don't!' said Natasha.

'The shit I don't!'

'Sergei, you drink it white with two sugars. Always!'

'Bah! Drink this way! Don't smoke that way! Shut the shit up, you bloody woman!'

Natasha shook her head slowly.

'I wash my hands of you . . .'

'Um, Sergei?' said Alan, interposing apologetically.

'Da?'

'Look, because we were running a bit late I thought it would be best if Ben went on and spoke to them on his own, but now that you're here I think we'll revert to the original plan. That is all right with you, is it?'

Philip shrugged.

'What you like. I don't give a shit.'

'Ah, right . . . So, um, if you'd like to wait here a moment, I'll just go out and introduce you, and please take your cue from me. Will that be OK, or would you prefer—'

'Just get on with it!'

Philip waved him away and away he went, through the unpainted swing-door.

'Don't you think you're overdoing this slightly?' Natasha whispered impatiently.

'No.'

He thought it had been a pretty spot-on impersonation thus far. Natasha began to say something more, but he waved her to silence.

'Ssh! I'm listening to my intro.'

Alan must have been standing just the other side of the door. They could hear every word:

'Ladies and gentlemen, we are doubly privileged today. Not just one major director has consented to honour us with his presence at our opening of the Stanislavsky Centre theatre, but two. Please give a very warm welcome to one of the most respected international dramaturges in world theatre today . . . Sergei Shustikov!'

Philip felt like a game-show contestant. Should he have bounced through the door, waving and grinning inanely? It was hardly in character. So instead he kicked open the door and barged in crossly.

'Sergei, please take a seat.'

Alan was putting a second barstool next to Ben's. Philip marched over. He was aware of Natasha slipping in behind him and settling herself unobtrusively at the side of the auditorium.

'Hi, it's great to meet you!' declared Ben Ferris warmly, seizing him by the hand. He seemed genuinely pleased to see him, as did the audience. Everyone was clapping enthusiastically. Philip took a good look around as he settled himself on to his stool. The audience was very young, students he guessed, either from the university or drama school, or both. He leered at some pretty girls in the front row.

'We're so, so lucky,' said Alan Fermon when the applause had died down, 'to have the directors of *the* two major current Shakespearian productions both here together under one roof – and they both happen to be of the same play! They've agreed to take questions from the floor and I'm sure we're in for some fascinating insights. Anyway, that's enough of me wittering – '

'Too damn right!' Philip grunted morosely.

'Er, yeah . . .' said Alan, thrown off his stride. 'Well, I'll get out the way then . . . Could we have a question to get the ball rolling? Yes – the red jumper.'

The red jumper belonged to a serious complexionally challenged youth; his face looked like a random assortment of pizza toppings.

'Could I ask,' asked red jumper, 'what political relevance do you think the Roman plays have in today's climate?'

Ben Ferris twisted round eagerly on his stool.

'I'm glad you asked that – '

'I'm not,' interrupted Philip.

Ben paid him no attention.

'I think we're witnessing the defragmentization of the centralized modern state,' explained the boy wonder intensely. 'I find the parallels frightening: not only do we have the resurgence of the political right mirrored in *Coriolanus*, but in *Julius Caesar* and *Antony and Cleopatra* I think we're dealing fundamentally with two halves of the same imperialist equation, demonstrating the essential gravitational pull of any autocracy, which is exactly the kind of situation we're seeing in former Yugoslavia today, whereby any attempt to escape the political orbit of a dictatorship is ruthlessly suppressed. That's why I chose a contemporary European setting. Admittedly the parallels are not exact, but I was also very aware during rehearsals, and I think it would be impossible for any director not to be, of a similar political process working itself out in

Russia at the present time. Perhaps Sergei would like to comment on that?'

'Like shit I would,' said Philip, who was looking around for an ashtray. There wasn't one, so he put his cigarette out in his half-drunk coffee. He doubted that it would impair the flavour.

'I've a question,' said one of the pretty girls in the front row.

'I've got a question too,' said an extremely grubby man in overalls who had just appeared through the door at the back.

'Yes?' said Philip, taking in the incongruous figure and mastering his surprise before anybody else. 'What is question?'

'My question is this,' the man answered in a strong local accent. 'Does anybody here own a blue Ford Granada? 'Cos if they do it's blocking our way out, and it's our dinner time.'

Natasha stood up.

'It's mine. I'm sorry. I'll come and move it.'

'Thanks very much, miss. Sorry to trouble you.'

Natasha and the workman went out together. The young woman at the front stuck up her hand again.

'Have you two seen each other's productions?'

There was a titter from the audience. Ben Ferris looked sheepish.

''Fraid I haven't had time yet. I look forward to it enormously though.'

'What about you, Sergei?' chipped in Alan Fermon from the edge of the stage.

Philip shrugged noncommittally.

'Yah. I see.'

'Really?' said Ben Ferris perkily. 'Oh well . . . what did you think?'

'Pile of shit.'

'I'm sorry?' Ben cocked his head, as if he hadn't heard.

'I said pile of shit,' Philip repeated with slow sadistic clarity. 'Clean shit ears out, Ferris.'

There was some nervous laughter from the audience. Ben joined in.

'What is shit laughing matter?' Philip growled at him. 'I ever produce shit like your shit I go hang myself.'

The laugh lines had all fled from Ben's face. Only a flush of redness gave character to the smooth bland cheeks.

'Er, perhaps we could have another question?' Alan Fermon suggested to the audience.

'What is wrong with this question?' Philip demanded, spinning round violently on his stool. 'She ask me damn good question, I give straight answer. What is meaning of this damn shit you give us, Ferris? I like to know!'

Philip turned back aggressively to face him. Ben looked completely stunned, much indeed as he had looked on the occasion of their last meeting backstage at the National Theatre.

'Don't you think this is a little gratuitous?' murmured the young director.

Philip stared at him coldly.

'Niet!'

Philip was aware of an electric tense expectancy in the audience. It was one of those rare theatrical moments when the collective breath seems stilled and the footfalls of mice resound like the charging of elephants. Philip savoured it deliciously.

'What is you do with damn shit play?' he demanded when he had sucked the last ounce of flavour from the moment. 'What is this shit about Russia, Bosnia, all that damn political shit waffling drivel crap? Have you read damn play, Ferris? Where did Shakespeare write all this damn bloody shit you give us?'

'I, I don't understand . . .' Ben gestured hopelessly. 'Are you complaining about the contemporary setting? Your production, as I understand it—'

'Bah!' Philip waved him away scornfully. 'We no talk about my shit production, is your shit production I mean. My production is red-hot shit hot, yours is like three-day-old dog turd. Where is passion? Where is sense Antony sacrifices world for love? What shit stupid idiot had idea of casting Dick Jones in part to start with?'

'Dick?' Ben gasped weakly. 'You can't be serious! Dick's one of the finest classical—'

'Shit bollocks, Ferris! Dick Jones is most useless talentless shit crap amateur actor in England. We are knowing this even in Vladivostock, for Christ sake! Not fit to cast as rear end of pantomime horse in shit-damn awful English so-called entertainment Christmas crap. Not just worse damn actor in country, worse damn actor in whole world. If damn Martians had shit shit-actor competition Jones is winner, every time! Why you give me this finest classical damn rubbish shit? Is not fit to kneel in shit and lick clean bootlaces of Philip Fletcher. Now there is genuine article! There is red-hot shit-hot damn fine classical actor if ever I see one, by God they are singing his praises even in Minsk. I come to England, I say "Get me Fletcher!" Any damn village-idiot director in Russia do exactly same thing. When I hear you cast Jones at shit Royal National Theatre I laugh! I think ha! This damn famous English sense of humour, or what? But when I see production I no laugh any more. I vomit in interval!'

It was not a speech to be delivered sitting down. Philip had leapt from his stool and was gesticulating with abandon, like an obstinate player determined to ignore the Prince of Denmark's stage directions.

'Bah!' he scowled, sawing the air with one last scornful gesture and dropping back heavily on to his stool. He swivelled round to face Alan. 'I have enough of this shit. What is time? I am here to open damn theatre, or not?'

'Er, yes, um . . .' Alan answered in a still small voice. He looked nervously at his watch. 'It's a little early, but . . .'

His voice trailed off as he registered the main door to the auditorium opening and heard voices outside.

'Um, come on in, please,' said Alan with his customary incisiveness.

Philip looked round impatiently. He had an almost pathological loathing for latecomers, whom he regarded as the Untouchables of the theatre-going breed, and this was one of the worst-designed theatres he'd ever seen for minimizing their disruptive effect: the large banked blocks of seating were inaccessible from the back, meaning that anyone coming in would have to skirt round to the front row before being able to take their place. From where he sat he couldn't see the entrance, but he could hear muttering voices.

'Get in! Get in!' he shouted impatiently towards where the voices were coming. 'Hurry the shit up!'

'Sergei, is that you?'

The voice that floated through to the front of the auditorium was tremulous and thin. It was like the voice of a ghost.

Shit! thought Philip, and he didn't have to be in character to think it.

'Sergei? I can't believe it!'

Nor could Philip. Nor would anyone in about two seconds' time. His cover was about to go through the roof.

He was off his stool and sprinting for the stage exit in one continuous movement. The door seemed a mile away. He was running through treacle, the shiny wooden floor stretched for ever, and it was giving way beneath him. No, it was he who was giving way, the motive power was all sucked from his limbs. He had lost his balance, he was falling. There was a shock of pain as his knees hit the ground and a burning sensation in his palms as he slewed to a halt. The voice of the ghost, much nearer now, cut sharply through his blurred senses.

'Sergei!' sobbed Melissa Pine. 'Talk to me, Sergei!'

He covered his head with his hands and thrust his face into the floor.

'Get the shit out of my life, you wretched woman!' he mumbled despairingly, while he prayed for a miracle.

'Sergei!' wailed Melissa, her voice and footsteps drawing ever closer. 'Sergei, you're alive!'

Alive? he thought. Call this living? Mountains and hills, come, come, and fall on me!

'You fucking bitch!' yelled Natasha at the top of her voice. 'How dare you show your face in here!'

There was a smack of flesh on flesh and Melissa yelped. Philip heard a heavy crash and felt the floorboards shake. He dared to sneak a furtive peep through his fingers. It was a scene of pure chaos:

Melissa was lying face down on the edge of the stage. Natasha was astride her, knees pressed into her shoulder blades, pummelling her face and head remorselessly. Superintendent Higginbottom was attempting to pull her off. It looked worse than Act V of *Hamlet*.

And there was a full supporting cast too, Philip noted, as he registered the shock on the faces of Ben Ferris and Alan Fermon, not to mention the thirty or so spear-carriers in the audience. At least no one would be able to complain afterwards about not getting full value for money.

'Get off her, miss!' Higginbottom was shouting as he tried to wrench Natasha away from Melissa. 'Let her go!'

But Natasha was clinging on like a limpet. Philip saw that the unpainted door at the back was still swinging gently on its springs. She must have returned from reparking her car in the nick of time.

'Thy hand, Great Anarch!' he murmured appreciatively as he pulled himself up on to his feet and prepared to make his bolt for freedom. Praise be to the goddess out of the machine!

'Mr Shustikov? I'd like a word, please!'

Philip glanced over his shoulder. The superintendent had both hands full trying to restrain Natasha. Philip shook his head.

'Catch me later, comrade!' he declared, and bolted for the exit.

He pushed the door back into place behind him and looked in vain for a lock. He hesitated. Getting out of immediate danger was one thing, but how to effect an escape? There was still the little matter of the body in the boot of the car, and Natasha was the one with the keys. He couldn't afford to go far.

His arm came into contact with the fire extinguisher on the wall bracket. There was a little square of glass next to it, bearing an injunction to break it in case of emergency. If this didn't classify as an emergency, then what did? He broke it with a sharp jab of his elbow.

Water came showering down on him from the ceiling. An

outburst of screaming from next door suggested that the whole sprinkler system had come into operation. At the same moment loud bells began to ring frantically. There would be a mass stampede for the exits any second now.

Philip darted behind the black curtains hanging down on the other side of the brick wall. He pressed his back into the brass plaque, ensured that the material covered his toes and made himself the tiniest of cracks to peep through. He didn't have long to wait.

The swing-doors were flung open and half a dozen members of the audience came streaming through. They dashed out through the gap in the wall. Superintendent Higginbottom came after them.

'Mr Shustikov?' he shouted from the door, holding his jacket above his head in a vain attempt to deflect the water from the sprinklers.

Philip declined to answer him.

'Stop that!' Higginbottom yelled suddenly, running back into the theatre. It wasn't hard for Philip to guess who he was shouting at: he could hear Melissa's screams even over the din of the alarm.

The members of the audience who had rushed out through the gap in the wall came rushing back in. Alan Fermon appeared at the door.

'We can't get out!' one of them told him. 'There's a car blocking the way.'

'Out the front with the others!' Alan ordered. 'Quick!'

He held the door for them and they ran on through. As the door fell back into place Philip heard the superintendent's voice:

'Stop that or I'll arrest you!'

Natasha shouted incoherently back at him. Melissa added her voice to the general gnashing.

The sprinklers were still going full blast. Philip kept the curtains tightly closed. He reckoned his was the only dry eye in the house.

'Out, everyone, out!' Alan was ordering shrilly. Higginbottom appeared at the door again.

'Where's Shustikov?'

'I don't bloody well know!' Alan answered crossly, materializing beside him. 'For heaven's sake, get out! The fire brigade'll be here any moment now!'

The distant hoot of sirens was added to the general cacophony. Philip knew that he wasn't going to be able to stay where he was for much longer. Nor, though, was anyone else.

'I said, stop that!' The superintendent yelled over his shoulder. He and Alan ran back into the theatre. There was a brief reprise of argumentative incoherence.

Natasha appeared at the door. She looked furious and was soaking wet. She ran through to the hole in the wall and stood outside in the dry, panting for breath. Philip opened the curtains and waved to her.

'What the hell are you doing?' she demanded angrily.

'Ssh!' he responded, indicating for her to come and join him.

'I'm not going back in there!' she answered defiantly, wringing out the damp hem of her skirt.

Philip cast a frantic glance towards the door.

'Where's Higginbotton?'

'Seeing to Melissa. Don't worry, they've gone out the front.'

'Thanks for telling me . . .'

He threw back the curtains and sprinted towards her. The pressure of water from the sprinklers was slackening off and he received only a light dousing.

'I'm going to catch a cold at this rate,' Natasha was muttering as he joined her. 'Did you do that?'

'Do what?'

'Set the fire alarm off, what do you think I meant?'

'Of course I did, and don't get ratty with me.'

'I saved your bacon in there, Philip, and my reward is a dose of double pneumonia.'

'It was only a cold a moment ago. I'm very grateful for your rescuing me. Are you sure about Higginbottom?'

'Of course I am. He had to go and get Melissa an ambulance.'

'I see.'

The sirens were drawing closer. So far they'd managed to get fire, ambulance and police. They'd be putting the 'House Full' sign up any minute now.

'We'd better get out of here,' he observed anxiously. 'Higginbottom'll be back.'

'I know. He's promised to arrest me.'

'Don't take it personally, it's just his job. Can we get the car out?'

'I don't see why not. I got it in.'

She'd reparked the Granada just to the right of them, flush between the concrete mixer and the corner of the building, the rear bumper almost touching the rope-line by the hole. It had been a smart piece of reversing, there was no room at all to squeeze past, as the fleeing audience members had discovered. It wasn't even possible to open the driver's door. Natasha threaded her way through the builders' debris to the passenger's side. Philip kept his eye on the hole in the wall, lest the superintendent return. He lit a cigarette to calm his nerves.

Natasha was squeezing herself through the door. What if Higginbottom saw them driving out, tried to stop them? He might succeed, the road was blocked, he had only to stand in front of the car. Perhaps he should lie on the floor . . .

'What the hell are you doing?' Philip demanded sharply.

Natasha was leaning over the passenger seat, reaching for something in the back.

'I'm getting a towel!' she answered crossly. 'I'm soaked!'

Their luggage was on the back seat. The boot, of course, was already occupied.

'Well hurry up,' Philip muttered back. 'We haven't got time to faff around . . .'

Perhaps the floor wasn't such a good place to hide after all. Higginbottom had only to glance in to spot him, and then he'd look pretty silly. There was always the boot. But the boot was occupied.

'Come on then!' said Natasha, who had at last squeezed herself into the driver's seat and was wiping her hair with her towel.

He went over to join her. The floor it would have to be. He dropped his cigarette, ground it out into a grey smear of cement that had spilled from the machine. Natasha turned on the engine.

'Give me the key!' he demanded suddenly, thrusting his hand at her through the open door.

'What?'

'Don't argue, just give me the key!'

The urgency in his voice must have impressed her. She turned off the engine and handed it over.

'Now get out. I'll need a hand.'

He ran round to the back of the car and checked the gap in the wall. He could see the door. Anyone coming through the door could see him. It was a big risk. No, it was more than that, it was an *insane* risk. He hesitated. Now he was the one who was faffing around. No time to waste weighing up the pros and cons, he told himself. What was it he'd said to Natasha about not committing actions unless you were prepared to live with the consequences? If you're going to do it, just do it . . . He inserted the car key in the boot lock.

'What are you up to?' Natasha demanded impatiently as she came clambering awkwardly over the passenger seat to join him.

'Hang on a second . . .'

He stepped over the rope-line and stared down into the hole in the ground. He picked up a loose half-brick and dropped it over the edge. It sank without trace in the thick goo of cement.

'Philip, are you thinking what I think you're thinking?'

'I think I may be. Open the boot.'

They stood together looking down at the corpse of her dead lover, an indistinct blanket-wrapped lump. Philip felt her slip her hand into his.

'We'll never get away with it,' she whispered.

'We've got away with it so far. Take his feet.'

Philip thrust his hands into the blanket and took a grip roughly under the armpits. Even with two of them it was hard getting the dead weight out of the car, but they knew all about that already. They handled the corpse like seasoned grave-robbers.

'Careful of the rope,' he warned, as he almost got caught up trying to lift his feet over. They staggered to the edge of the hole.

'On the count of three . . .'

He checked over his shoulder. If Higginbottom should choose to reappear through the theatre door in the next few moments then they were done for. Or what if the workmen returned suddenly from lunch? Don't think about it, he told himself again, just do it! Do it! Do it!

'One, two, three . . .'

They flung the body away from them with all their strength. It travelled in the narrowest of graceless arcs before falling head first into a vertical plummet. They stood watching silently, panting for breath and nursing their wrenched arms.

There was a sound like the smack of a wet towel on skin as Sergei's head hit the cement. The shoulders and upper torso disappeared instantly from sight, leaving the waist and legs poking out from the blanket and sticking up into the air. For one ghastly second the lower body hung there, apparently stuck, but then, with heart-stopping slowness, it began to list to one side and to slip by inches into the thick setting concrete. For a long last theatrical moment one large booted foot remained thrusting into the air, then it too vanished into the opaque grey depths, twisting round in a final flourish like Poseidon bidding a playful farewell to the Argonauts.

The area round where he had sunk was as blistered as a moonscape, but already the viscous sludge was flowing in to fill up the tiny craters. In half a minute there would be nothing to attract the casual eye to Sergei's last resting place. And there wasn't ever going to be much likelihood of a passing dog sniffing him out.

The sound of sirens drew nearer. With luck they'd go to the front of the building, but if they came round the back then the car was going to be boxed in again.

'Let's get back to London,' he suggested to Natasha. 'We've a show to do tonight.'

She retrieved the keys from the boot. He stopped her in the act of closing it.

'I'd better not be seen with you,' he told her. 'I'll get in.'

'If you insist.'

He climbed over the bumper and settled himself down between the spare tyre and the tool kit.

'Please drive carefully,' he pleaded. As she slammed the lid on him she promised that she would.

He lay in the uncomfortable darkness trying to ignore the faint odour of decay and the car's violent joltings. As they turned out into the main road he heard a siren flash past. He listened to it fading in the distance, a last excursion and alarm as the curtain came down on the end of Act II.

Only the small matter of the epilogue remained.

# 17

The Sunday night 8 p.m. ferry-sailing from Boulogne to Dover was delayed because of an incident.

The incident had occurred on the outward voyage, and had come to light when a travelling member of the public handed in a black leather holdall which he said he had found outside on the upper deck. A tannoy announcement was made just as the ship came in to dock:

'Would Mr Sergei Shustikov please report to the purser's office to collect his luggage.'

As the holdall contained not merely clothes but also money, a return ticket and a passport, the purser was confident that Mr Shustikov would be along shortly to reclaim his property. If he was the same 'Russian gentleman' who had been reported to him earlier (as seemed likely) then he would take the opportunity to have a few sharp words with him.

'He's reduced two of my girls to tears!' the highly agitated chief steward had burst in to tell him half an hour earlier. 'And as for his language, sir! Even after twenty years at sea I'm shocked!'

It seemed there had been a contretemps in the bar. The Russian had clearly had a few too many and the bar staff had refused to serve him another. He had become seriously abusive.

'It was shit this and shit that, sir,' the chief steward reported. 'I've never heard so much shit!'

The purser had had a word with security and warned them to keep a look-out for an inebriated Russian, but nothing more had been heard of him.

And nor was anything heard of him again. When he failed to turn up to collect his luggage the purser ordered a search of the ship and detailed two of his officers to keep an eye on the disembarking passengers. No drunken Russian was among them. When the search party returned empty-handed the purser began to fear the worst. He spoke to the captain, and the captain spoke to the coastguard. Shortly afterwards the word went out to vessels in the Channel to keep a watch out for a suspected man overboard.

No one paid any attention to a dark-haired man in sunglasses of about the Russian's build and age who was among the first to leave the ship. He had gone straight to the disembarkation queue after handing in the black leather holdall containing the Russian's possessions.

Once through the non-existent customs check the dark-haired man made for the nearest taxi rank. The cabbie was a little surprised to be asked to drive to the rival ferry-port of Calais, but he supposed that an eccentric Englishman's money was as good as anyone's. At the end of a slightly scenic hour-long drive he deposited his passenger at the Calais ferry terminal.

Some two hours later the man arrived back in England and boarded the train to London. From Victoria station he took a cab to Highbury.

Philip Fletcher arrived home in the small hours of Monday morning.

When *Antony and Cleopatra* closed at the Riverside Studios after an immensely successful six-week run there was talk of a West End transfer. Seymour Loseby did not think that it would happen.

'Why ever not?' his friend demanded incredulously, handing over a glass of port and lemon. Seymour indicated the other end of the crowded bar with a nod of the head.

'Because of your lookalike.'

'Philip Fletcher?' His friend took a sip of his Guinness as he tried to identify the leading actor among the throng. 'He can't still be upset about the reviews, can he?'

'You must be joking! If I know Philip he'll be festering for at least another six months.'

'But you said the audiences were loving him. I thought Fletcher would leap at the chance of swanning about on Shaftesbury Avenue, especially now Ben Ferris's production is coming off.'

'Ah yes . . .' Seymour chuckled. 'Houses have been at about forty percent, haven't they? I don't suppose Dick Jones is amused.'

'No. Amused is not a word I would use to describe him.'

'Oh dear oh dear.' Seymour chuckled again, with menace. 'They're a fickle lot are Joe and Josephina Public. Mind you, I think that's one reason Philip doesn't want to go on. As he says, the audiences have only been coming since all the publicity about Shitski's disappearance. Ours has obviously become the "in" *Ant and Cleo* to see, but the novelty's bound to wear off soon. I think Philip's being canny. Once audiences start noticing the production rather than the hype the collective enthusiasm will begin to dim. The other reason he doesn't want to go on at the moment is he's talking about setting up his own company.'

'Him too?'

'Yes, they're all at it, aren't they?'

'The publicity hasn't done Fletcher any harm, has it?'

'Not after what Shitski said about him in Bristol got into the papers.'

'I saw Dick Jones reading it up in the National bar the day after.'

'I don't suppose he looked too happy.'

'Happy is another word I wouldn't use to describe him.'

'Neither happy nor amused? What a sorry little bunny he must be!'

'Apparently he was furious with Ferris for not sticking up for him. And the beauty was that Jones couldn't do a damned thing about it. It would have looked like speaking ill of the dead.'

'Ah! They never found Shitski's body . . .'

'They never found Amelia Earhart's either, but I think we can assume. What was he doing on that ferry in the first place?'

'He was probably emigrating. He never stopped complaining about this country. Mind you, I don't suppose he'd have liked anywhere else any better.'

'Odd chap, eh?'

'I'll say. Had this knack of just pushing off, going "walk-about", as Natasha puts it. Do you really think we dare believe the old monster isn't going to turn up again some day? I'm not sure I could stand the shock if he did.'

'I don't suppose you're the only one. Where's Natasha Fielding?'

'Isn't she at the bar?'

'No. Philip Fletcher is, though.'

'Why have you adopted that insinuating tone of voice?'

'They're quite friendly, aren't they?'

'They've known each other for years.'

'If rumour is to be believed, they are an item.'

'Is that so?'

'Come off it, Seymour.'

'My lips are sealed.'

'Like a feeding whale's.'

'Very like a whale's.'

'So you admit that they're an item?'

'I admit no such thing.'

'Yet by your smile you seem to say so.'

'You have an overactive imagination. Now for heaven's sake put it on a leash – Philip's coming over.'

'Does that mean I have to tell him he was wonderful?'

'I should if I were you . . . Philippo! How goes it, troth?'

'Frankly, I'm knackered.'

'Verily though speak'st sooth. You know each other?'

Seymour indicated his friend, who lifted his glass of Guinness in salute to Philip.

'By reputation. Saw the show again tonight. Excellent. Well done.'

Philip gave a modest bow before turning his attention to Seymour.

'We're all going back to your place, I understand.'

'A trifling, foolish banquet. You didn't make it last time, did you?'

'Last time?'

'We repaired *chez moi* after the first night. You were on guard duty as I recall.'

Seymour explained matters to his friend:

'*Pauvre* Philippe ended up minding Shitski. Even put him to bed on his sofa. Amazingly forbearing, if I may say so.'

Philip sighed.

'Poor Sergei. It was a pretty awful way to go.'

'You're sure he's gone? We were just discussing the possibility that he might turn up hale and hearty after all.'

'I think you can discount that.'

'You sound very sure, Philip.'

'I feel it in my bones, Seymour.'

'Ah, dem bones, dem bones, dem wet bones.'

'Still, Sergei is set to achieve at least a degree of immortality. You've heard that they're going to rename the new theatre in Bristol in his honour? At last Stanislavsky will be eclipsed by Shustikov.'

'Yes, Natasha did mention something.'

'She's going down to do the business next week. She's asked me to go with her. Not sure if I'll be able to.'

'She may need protection from the police, Philip. Didn't they threaten to arrest her last time?'

'Oh, they're always threatening to arrest people. They seem to think it's what they're there for.'

'At least your friend from Bath has stopped hanging round.'

'Alas, poor Higginbottom.'

'And poor Melissa.'

'Poor, poor Melissa.'

'Still in the loony bin, is she?'

'I think they call it a sanatorium, Seymour.'

'Call it what you will, dear, the poor thing's barking. And so will I be, soon, if I don't get another drink. Shall we repair for Egyptian bacchanals at Château Loseby?'

'It sounds suitably decadent. I'll get Natasha.'

'Where is she?'

'In her dressing room. I think she had a bit of a headache.

Nothing serious, I'm sure she'll be delighted to come on. I'll go and find her.'

Philip did not notice the knowing look exchanged between Seymour and his friend; he was on so high an ego-trip that the doings of lesser mortals barely registered. He tailed off breezily towards the Studio Theatre and knocked lightly on Natasha's door. She was reclining on the sofa.

'Headache better?'

She nodded.

'Good.'

He knelt down and kissed her hungrily.

'I've been wanting to do that for the past half hour,' he murmured into her ear. 'I'd better get my ration in, seeing as we still have to behave in public. Are you sure you're all right?'

'Yes. I'm much better.'

'You don't sound it. I know this charade's a hell of a strain, but I think we should keep it up a bit longer. You know how suspicious the police are: if it gets back to Higginbottom that we've been having an affair he'll never believe I didn't do away with Sergei. We've got to be discreet. Now let's go. We don't want to miss Seymour's party again, he'll think us terribly rude.'

'Philip, there's something I've got to tell you.'

'Can't it wait?'

'I've got to tell you some time.'

'All right.' He got up off the floor and dusted down his knees. 'Be my guest.'

'Would you mind not smoking, please?'

He had just taken out his cigarettes. He paused in the act of opening his matches.

'Is anything the matter?' he asked indulgently, not lighting the cigarette but not putting it away either.

'Why should it be? I just asked you if you wouldn't mind not smoking, that's all.'

'You've never objected before.'

He took a match out of the box and made to strike it. She snatched it away crossly.

'Philip, it's no big deal, you know. I'm not asking you to

give up, just not to smoke when you're with me. That's not too much to ask, is it?'

'Whatever is the matter?'

'Look, will you stop asking me what's the matter? Nothing's the matter, I just don't want to breathe in your smoke. I don't want to make a big thing of it, OK?'

'But that's precisely what you are doing. Why are you being so obsessive?'

'Philip, it's unhealthy!'

'For me, maybe —'

'Haven't you ever heard of passive smoking?'

'For Christ's sake, Natasha, you're not in California now!'

'Perhaps this isn't the right time to talk after all. You go on ahead if you want to.'

'What, without you?'

'As you say, perhaps we shouldn't be seen arriving together.'

'Just because you give me a lift doesn't mean you're sleeping with me! I do think that's a bit of an over-reaction. Well, I don't know . . . Perhaps I'm being unduly cautious. Perhaps we can say tonight's the night it happened. Six weeks isn't very long, I know, it's only delicate to leave a brief mourning period for Sergei, however undeserved, but the longer we keep it secret the harder it becomes. And it'll get worse – at least we've had an excuse for seeing each other up till now. It might be safer if we discreetly let it out into the open. You can say you turned to me for support, we're old friends, it's perfectly reasonable, then one thing led to another, we might even plant a sympathetic story in the gossip columns. Yes, that's a good idea, I wonder if we could get someone to give Nigel Dempster a call, then we can date the beginning of our relationship officially from – well, you'd better be the judge of that, we don't want anyone to think you're easy —'

'It's a bit late for that, Philip. I'm pregnant.'

'Well, maybe we should leave it . . . a month . . . a month, yes . . . what did you just say?'

'I'm pregnant.'

'You're pregnant?'

'Yes.'

'You mean you're going to have a baby?'

'That is what it usually means.'

'Give birth?'

'I think you've exhausted all the synonyms.'

'Bloody hell, I need a cigarette . . .'

'Philip, I did ask you not to smoke—'

'You must be joking!'

His knees had suddenly given way. He grabbed for the nearest chair and slumped down on to it in a state of near shell-shock. She sat up on the sofa and drew her knees up defensively. As he exhaled his first puff she made to wave away the smoke.

'Don't you think you're exaggerating just a *soupçon*?' he enquired drily.

'It's not my health I'm worried about, it's the baby. Philip, you've got to behave responsibly.'

He had never behaved responsibly in his life. It was much too late to start now.

'But . . .' he gestured limply. 'How long have you known?'

'Only since this morning. I did a test on myself earlier in the week. Went to the doctor straight away, she confirmed it today. I didn't mean to tell you like this.'

'But . . . how did it happen?'

'That's a very naive question.'

'I wasn't asking you to draw me a diagram, for Christ's sake!'

'Don't shout, Philip.'

'I'm sorry, I'm a bit . . . on edge. This is all very unexpected. I don't know what to say. Look, I hope this doesn't sound insulting, but – you're sure I'm the father?'

'Quite sure.'

He closed his eyes and put his head in his hands. It was too much for him to take in all at once. How on earth had it happened? It had never happened before. If women were going to start getting pregnant on him it would completely ruin his sex life.

Natasha waved with irritation at some invisible smoke.

'Philip, we've got to think this through properly.'

'I know,' he answered miserably. He had been feeling pleasantly amorous until about five minutes ago, but his libido had just crashed through the floor. He doubted that he would ever dare go near a female again unless he were sheathed from head to toe in reinforced latex.

'I'm about six weeks' pregnant. It may even have happened our first night together, in Bristol. That might look bad, Philip.'

Worse than bad; it would look suspicious. The awful implications were only just beginning to sink in.

'I hope your doctor's discreet. We'd better get you to a clinic, fast.'

'A clinic?'

'Well, you can't have the baby, obviously —'

'Are you suggesting I have an abortion?'

'Don't get het up. I'll pay for it.'

'You bastard!'

The blow she landed on the side of his face took him completely by surprise. She hit him so hard he fell off the chair, his cigarette flying out of his mouth and into the corner. He lay in a heap on the floor, staring up at her dumbly.

'Something I said?'

She had leapt off the sofa and was standing over him. She was bristling.

'You really are the most selfish bastard I've ever met! You know perfectly well how much having a baby means to me. How could you even suggest that I have an abortion? I must have been mad to choose you for a father!'

She was probably right. Of everyone he had ever met in his entire life he couldn't think of a single candidate less suited to fatherhood. He had such a negative paternal instinct that he had sometimes wondered if he might not actually be allergic to children. Other people's were bad enough; the thought of producing one of his own was intolerable. He nodded his head keenly.

'Well if you'd asked me first I would have agreed with you.'

'I didn't have time to ask you first, you bloody fool!'

'Well I . . . Hang on, what did you just say? . . . You don't mean . . . Oh no, I think you do . . .'

A shining light had penetrated his mental darkness. He almost heard the ratchety noise as his brain clunked at last into gear.

'My God . . . you really did choose me, didn't you? You did it deliberately . . .'

He got up slowly, rubbing his aching cheek. He could feel the quickening pulse of blood in his temple.

'I never could work you out, I never did understand how you kept yourself going. One minute you were a nervous wreck, the next you were more in control than I was. It was a brilliant piece of acting, but what was your motive? That's the thing I couldn't get, the key to the whole performance. Well, I've got it now, haven't I, and the joke's on me. "Don't worry about that!" you murmured in my ear in that bloody motel room. "I've taken care of everything." Oh yes, and very good care too. With your attitude to contraception you should get a medal from the Pope!'

'All right, Philip, I may have been careless. We had a lot on our minds, remember? As you had the delicacy to remind me, one false step and there'd have been no shopping trips to Mothercare for me.'

'Oh but they have excellent crèche facilities in Holloway these days, don't they? And if they were going to bang you up at least you'd make sure you had the consolation of my banging you up first!'

'Philip, don't be crude.'

'It's a bit late to go all prim on me now, Natasha. We've not just drawn the diagram, we've done the bloody practical. And bingo, it's a bullseye! I can't believe how devious you've been. You thought this up from the start, didn't you? I see it all, my God I see it all . . . You even wanted a quick one while Sergei's corpse was still warm over there on the sofa! You've been using me all along!'

'You used me!'

'Ah, so you don't deny it! Just what the hell are we meant to do now? If the baby pops out right on time in seven and a

185

half months it's not going to take a mathematical genius to work out that we must have been on frankly intimate terms at exactly the same moment old Sergei conveniently did his vanishing act. How do you think Higginbottom will react to that? For heaven's sake, Natasha, this is a disaster!'

'Not necessarily.'

'You're thinking of passing the conception off as immaculate, are you?'

'No. I shall say that Sergei was the father.'

'What?'

'No one need know that you had anything to do with it, and, to be quite honest, after the way you've been behaving tonight, that might very well be for the best. Philip, you've just put a cigarette out, you shouldn't light up another one —'

'O most pernicious woman! Cease and desist!'

He was feeling giddy, he had to sit down again. He sucked on his cigarette defiantly. A woman was only a woman, but a filter-tipped Virginia was one of his few remaining handles on reality. He was in a state of terrible shock. His life had just been turned completely inside out; then upside down; then torn into little pieces; then all the little pieces had been scattered into the ether, leaving him feeling like he'd been shredded. All the assumptions he had made about himself and Natasha had been dynamited. He'd actually cared about her; he'd been serious about a woman for the first time since . . . the last time. He couldn't remember, that wasn't the point, the point was that he was hurt. Selfish bastard, she'd called him. What did that make her? He'd been sacrificed on the altar of her grand obsession.

'I don't think you've treated me very fairly!' he complained.

'Don't sulk, Philip, it's pathetic.'

'But what about us? I thought we had something together?'

'Stop sounding like a B-movie. We do have something together. But now another something has come along that's bigger than both of us.'

'I think I prefer my B-movie to yours.'

'Only because you get to star in it.'

He hesitated. Perhaps she was right. He probably was a

selfish bastard. Wasn't everybody? He was just more up-front about it than most people. But if he had an ego problem, he wasn't the only one. As ruthless solipsists went, she must have been pretty close to scoring a perfect ten. He had been warned; he'd walked into the trap with his eyes open. Anyway, what kind of a relationship could two dedicatedly self-obsessed people expect to have together?

Two stars keep not their motion in one sphere . . .

It was still a bit much, though: telling him he was going to be a father one minute, then informing him she would pretend it was someone else's the next. And not just anybody else's, but the man's she had murdered. Talk about chutzpah! She really was extraordinary. He felt unable to contain his admiration.

'What are you going to call the child?'
'Something Shakespearian. What do you think of Cordelia?'
'I meant the surname.'
'She'll use mine. I merely intend to acknowledge Sergei, there's no need to perpetuate him. Cordelia Fielding, what do you think?'
'A little over-dramatic.'
'Perdita? Or Marina? Yes, I like Marina.'
'What if it's a boy?'
'I want a daughter.'
He smiled wryly, and declaimed:

Bring forth men-children only:
For thy undaunted mettle should compose
Nothing but males . . .

'It's very bad form, Philip, to quote from the Scottish play, you should know that. It's also a very chauvinist sentiment.'
'My dear,' he murmured softly. 'There's nothing politically correct about *me* . . . A Shakespearian name, eh? In view of her parentage, perhaps we should call her Lady Macbeth.'

She returned his smile knowingly. She came over and stroked the cheek she had slapped.

'Perhaps you weren't such a bad choice after all.'

She sat down on his lap and kissed him. She started to unbutton his shirt.

'I thought you'd got what you came for?' he said.

'That was business, this is pleasure. And besides, I did want you, you know . . .'

There was a sharp rapping at the door.

'Damn!' muttered Philip. 'Why does this always happen to us?'

'Natasha? Philip?' cooed Seymour's voice from behind the door. 'We're off to the party. Are you coming?'

'Not if you have anything to do with it,' Philip murmured under his breath, rebuttoning his shirt. Natasha got up off his lap and went to answer the door.

'We'll be along in a sec,' she told him.

'Oh good! Would it be all right if my friend and I cadged a lift?'

'Of course . . .'

She picked up her things. Philip helped her into her coat.

'Ready, dears?' urged Seymour from the corridor. 'I don't want my guests to arrive before me. Let's go!'

'We're ready.'

'Then let us depart.'

And they departed, the Captains and the Queens, the actors and the actorines, stars and aspirants and mechanicals and camp followers in various senses, each playing their part, and several several, though none with more varied splendour than Philip Fletcher, without doubt the finest talent of his generation. Without doubt as far as he was concerned, at any rate. The fact that so many people at Seymour's kept telling him how wonderful he was only confirmed his own impression.

Some hours later Seymour's friend, who had drunk rather more Guinness than was politic in a man of his advanced years and limited bladder control, buttonholed him in the corridor of his flat and invited him to peer through the door of the spare bedroom, unwisely left ajar. In the corner Philip Fletcher and Natasha Fielding were snogging and groping each other like a pair of randy teenagers.

'Try denying they're an item now!' his friend whispered salaciously in his ear.

'Well I won't tell anyone if you won't.'

But he did. And later, when everyone had gone home, Seymour even wrote about it in his diary, but that, as they say, is another story.